C.5

Danger in Disguise

Mary Alice Downie

John Downie

Cover Illustration by Carol Biberstein

ROUSSAN
PUBLISHERS INC.
Specializing in YA and fiction for pre-teens

THE CANADA COUNCIL | LE CONSEIL DES ARTS
FOR THE ARTS | DU CANADA
SINCE 1957 | DEPUIS 1957

We acknowledge the support of the Canada
Council for the Arts for our publishing program.

We acknowledge the financial support of the Government
of Canada through the Book Publishing Industry
Development Program (BPIDP) for our publishing activities.

http://www.roussan.com

Copyright ©2000 by Mary Alice Downie

National Library of Canada
Bibliothèque nationale du Québec

Canadian Cataloguing in Publication Data

Downie, Mary Alice, 1934-
Danger in disguise

(On time's wing)
ISBN 1-896184-72-3

1. Québec Campaign, 1759--Juvenile fiction.
I. Title. II. Series.
PS8557.O85D35 2000   jC813'.54   C00-900201-4
PZ7.D75924Da 2000

Cover design by Dan Clark
Interior design by Jean Shepherd

Typeface Sabon 10.9

Published simultaneously in Canada and the United States of America
Printed in Canada

2 3 4 5 6 7 8 9 HLN 9 8 7 6 5 4 3 2

For Sam and Matilda

Contents

Maps

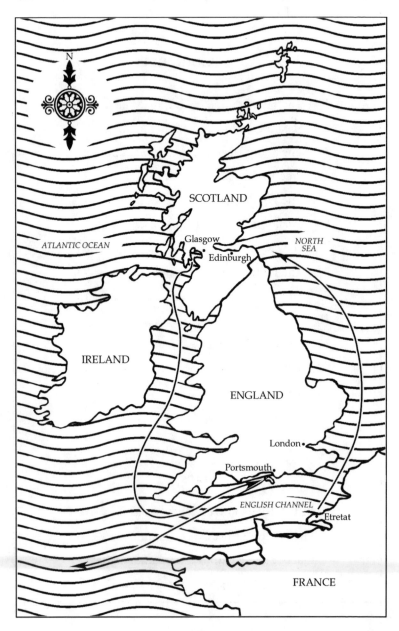

BRITISH ISLES AND NORMANDY COAST

1
The Hunter

January 1759

"Double-six!" Jamie picked up his last four stones from the board and started to lay them out again quickly, hoping for another game.

"That is all for tonight," said his father. "I can't match your luck on your birthday."

He reached for the jug of water, half-filled the iron pot and swung it over the fire. "We'll need more wood if I'm to enjoy a toddy before you go to bed."

"Are you expecting a visitor?"

"Why do you ask?"

"You've been watching time by the candle and listening to the wind," Jamie replied.

His father smiled. "I must be more careful if you are going to be so observant. No, I don't expect anyone tonight. I just have a restless feeling."

"I hope that doesn't mean we'll be moving on again," Jamie said. "I like this village. I've made friends here."

His father poked the fire, sending a shower of flames and sparks up the chimney. Jamie saw his shadow grow large on the wall and blur in the flickering light. The brass lock on the chest glowed, then vanished as though the chest were a huge one-eyed cat sitting in the dark. As Jamie watched, the great beast opened its glowing eye and glared at him.

"Fetch the wood before we lose the fire."

His father had never explained why they moved suddenly from place to place in France. Once in a while he would start to talk about the past and their home in Scotland, but then he would stop abruptly, and say, "Later, Jamie, later, when you are older."

Jamie stood up and pulled on his jacket to go out for the wood. If he wasn't old enough now, when would he be?

"Why do we keep moving?" he demanded. "Are we running away from something?"

His father looked up from the fire, surprised by the determined tone of the question. "Well, you are fourteen now, and a young man. I suppose I have to stop thinking of you as a child." His smile transformed his worn face. "I had better start taking you into my confidence and asking for the odd bit of advice. I'm not very good at that, am I? Never have been, for that matter." He looked back at the dying fire and began to speak as if recalling a dream.

"We have been running away—from a man who wants to kill us both. His name is Sleat. He is rich and powerful.

And on the subject of Duncan and Jamie Macpherson he is quite mad."

Jamie stood absolutely still, afraid to make any sound which would make his father stop talking.

"It began in Glasgow years ago, when I was studying the Law. It's an old story—a poor young girl betrothed by her bankrupt father to a rich man she despises. Unfortunately for Sleat, I was in love with her too and she with me. I did what I considered to be the only honourable thing. I rescued her on her wedding day and took her off to the Highlands."

Jamie strained to hear the low words. He had never thought of his father as ever being young; this stern red-haired man who spent most of his days hunched over account books for Gaston Leblanc, when he wasn't scolding Jamie for covering his Latin book with drawings. Jamie looked at him with new respect.

His father studied the dying embers, oblivious to the cold that had crept into the room. "Once we were safely with my clan in the north, we settled down to begin a long, happy, married life. It was happy but it was not fated to be long. The fiery cross summoned the clans to battle, and my chief sent me to fight against the English. The war went well at first and then, as you know from all the tales you have heard from my Jacobite friends, it turned into a disaster. After the battle of Culloden we were scattered to the winds and hunted down like wild beasts."

His deep voice intoned the words like a lament.

"I was hiding in the hills with my chief, Cluny

Macpherson. You and your mother were in the glen with the women and children of the clan. Then the English soldiers came. They burned the houses and took the animals from the farms, while the people starved in the ruins. Young and old were driven from shelter and many died. When word reached me, I left immediately for the glen but I was too late to save your mother. You were only a year old, a strange bundle for a fugitive Highlander to carry when fleeing from his enemies, but we survived.

"Later, when we were trying to start a new life in France, I learned that Sleat had taken part in the raids on the glens. He discovered through his spies that we had escaped, and when he heard where we were living he came to kill us. But I had been warned by friends and we escaped once more. Every time we found a new place to settle, the hunt began again."

"But why do we run away?" asked Jamie, shifting from one foot to the other with excitement. "You always tell me to stand up and fight for my rights."

His father looked up from the fire with a flash of anger on his face. "Sleat is too clever. He only fights when he is certain to win. He challenged my brother Malcolm to a duel in Scotland, but when Malcolm proved to be the better swordsman, Sleat called on his men and they killed him. So until I can make it a fair fight I must swallow my pride and run.

"Don't look so sad, Jamie. The days of running are almost over. You are big enough to be my ally now. Besides, Sleat hasn't found us yet in this desolate corner of the world."

He drew a short knife from the top of his boot. "I made the backgammon board last night when you were asleep and didn't quite finish the job. I'll cut your initials in one corner and your age in the other. It isn't every day you turn fourteen."

Jamie handed him the board, still trying to understand the unexpected torrent of words in answer to his question. He decided not to risk asking more at the moment. It had been a good birthday. His father had cut his lessons short "to celebrate." Then at supper he'd produced the backgammon game. "The folding board will fit in your pack," he'd said. "In case we have to move on."

Jamie sighed. At least now he knew why they kept moving. First they'd lived in Paris, then Dunkirk, Rouen, Fécamp, and finally this fishing village with its pebbly bay protected by soaring white cliffs. He stepped outside and the wind cut his face like a hundred tiny knives. Snow covered the rooftops of the clustered houses. Here and there a light burned cheerfully in a window, and from one house danced the sound of fiddlers. The Leblancs had sailed home with a good catch that morning, and he knew what a good catch meant in this part of the country.

"Best smugglers on the Normandy coast," was his friend Gilles' boast.

It was cold. Jamie blew on his fingers and loaded his arms with logs from the woodpile. The snow fell gently, covering his head and shoulders. He shook the soft wet flakes from his hair and turned to go back to the cottage. A black shadow detached itself from the wall and a man stepped silently in front of him. Jamie dropped the wood and reached for one of the logs.

"Easy now," said the shadow with a dry chuckle. "Your father's son, I see, but you needn't be so quick to defend yourself. I'm a friend. Go in and tell your father that Andrew Cameron is here with word from Paris. I've no wish to surprise him as well. I'll bring the wood," he added.

Jamie burst into the cottage. "Father, there's a stranger. He calls himself Andrew Cameron. Says he brings news from Paris."

Duncan Macpherson rose from his seat by the fire. "Bid him enter, lad. He is a friend indeed."

Before Jamie could deliver his message, Cameron came through the doorway, bent double to avoid its low lintel, with a great pile of logs under one arm. He dropped the logs by the hearth and shook the snow from his cloak. Then he greeted Duncan, introduced himself to Jamie again, and settled his lanky frame on the stool by the fire.

"When they told me you were well hidden, they didn't exaggerate. I had the devil of a time to find you."

"Did anyone follow you?"

"Now, Duncan, what are you saying?" A broad grin creased his craggy face. "Did anyone ever follow a Cameron when he didn't want to be followed? But, no matter. Sleat's men have found out where you are, and that's why I'm here tonight. They'll be here by morning."

"Then we'll have to disappoint them again," Jamie's father said, looking at Jamie. "I was planning to leave soon anyway. I must go to Paris and then tend to a little business in the Highlands."

"The man's daft," Cameron informed Jamie. "If they catch him in Scotland, they'll hang him quicker than snow melts in the river."

"And if I stay here they'll shoot me," Jamie's father said cheerfully. He ladled the boiling water into three large mugs and added a spoonful of honey to each. "Pass me the jug," he said to Jamie. "The water of life, all the way from Skye." He pulled the cork, threw it into the fire, then poured a little into Jamie's mug and a generous portion into the other two. He handed the mugs to his friend and son and took a long swig from his own.

"Well, Jamie, you'll be packing your board even sooner than I expected. We leave tomorrow, but not together. We must follow separate paths for a while. You will leave on the morning tide. Gaston's brother's boat is loaded and ready to sail. He'll put you ashore on the coast of Scotland. Then you must make your way to your Uncle Archie's house in Glasgow. He'll keep you safe until I finish my work in the Highlands. I'll come for you in the spring and we'll sail for Virginia to start a new life."

"You make it sound like a stroll in the park," Andrew Cameron objected. "Does the boy know that you'll both be hunted men in Scotland, fit only for a redcoat's bayonet or a hangman's rope? Your faithful enemy Sleat cherishes his grievances dearly." He looked hard at Jamie. "I don't know what you understand of all this, my boy, but I've been a friend of your father for more years than I care to count, and the old fox is so secretive that I fear you know little and understand less."

"I didn't know I had an uncle." Jamie blurted.

His father's face flushed with embarrassment. "Why burden him with the past?" he mumbled. "I've had enough to do stuffing Latin and mathematics into his thick head."

"Worse than I suspected," Andrew Cameron said. "Just look at the man. You can't tell his red beard from his red hair with all that shame on his face."

"Archie Gilchrist is your mother's brother," he told Jamie. "He never blamed her for running away with this wild Highlander, although it caused him a deal of trouble with Sleat. Your uncle is a hard man but a fair one, and he will stand by you. He made a fortune in the tobacco trade, and if anyone can protect you against Sleat he can. But first you have to reach him."

Jamie smiled broadly. "That sounds fine. When do we start?"

Andrew Cameron groaned and shook his head. "I should have expected this. Like father, like son. Well, they say God protects fools and drunk men. You have your father's faith in miracles. Do you also have his wits to help them happen?

"Come, Andrew, don't be so serious," said Jamie's father. "He may be only a boy, but he's healthy and I've given him some schooling. It hasn't all been tales of clan glories. He's well-spoken in English, French, and the Gaelic. So what he doesn't know he can ask about, and if he can just learn to listen more than he talks, he'll manage fine."

"How will I know my uncle?" Jamie asked, trying to change the subject.

Cameron swallowed his toddy. "Archie will be strutting about the town as usual in his bushy wig, red cloak and gold-topped cane. Anyone in Glasgow will point you the way to the grand house of Master Archibald Gilchrist, the Tobacco Lord. It's by the Trongate. Can you remember that?" He hesitated. "If you have any trouble, just ask for Willie the Ferret."

"Who is he?" Jamie asked. "Is he an uncle too?"

Both men laughed and refilled their mugs.

"Willie works for your uncle and is known everywhere. But be discreet when you ask for him. He has many friends and if they think you mean him mischief, you might not last the night.

"You will recognize him if you think of a ferret. You know that fierce little creature that slinks as it walks and suddenly stares at you?"

Jamie nodded. One of the boys in the village had one.

"Willie's eyes miss nothing. He has a thin face and a long pointed nose. When he looks at you, you will feel like a rabbit fixed by the bright beady gaze of a ferret. He's a good friend and a bad enemy. You'll know him, I promise you!"

Andrew Cameron stretched and yawned, then stood up, went to the door and looked out. The street lay deserted in the moonlight, silent under the snow.

"We must go before Sleat's men come pounding on the door."

"They'll not be here before morning. I've had dealings with those rogues before." Duncan lifted down his sword from over the fireplace and started to gather his belongings.

Jamie knew they wouldn't spend much time packing. They'd developed that to a fine art. He began to move about the room, collecting his treasures. They were few enough: the pocket knife that he'd found on the beach and honed to a gleaming sharpness, a shirt, two books that his father had given him, and his grandfather's dirk.

He listened to his father singing quietly as he prepared to leave:

> The lady came riding in the land,
> With four-and-twenty at her command;
> She was the bravest in the land
> And she followed a beggar man.

How many more times he would hear "The Gaberlunzie Man," which his father always sang before a sudden departure to a new place and a new life. He looked around the room where they had spent the last year. It was cold and bare, with only two chairs, a stool and a rough table, but he had been happy here. Andrew had already taken the chest out to be loaded onto his father's horse. The jug was empty. He thought about the months ahead. He hoped he would be brave and not bring dishonour to his name, and he repeated the Macpherson motto to encourage himself: "Touch not the cat without a glove."

"What are you muttering, lad?" asked Andrew Cameron. "Come, man, we must be off, You'll scarce have time to make your farewells."

"Leave-takings are best brief anyway," said Duncan. "Jamie, tell Gaston the time has come for us to go. He's been expecting it and the arrangements have already been made."

He took a small moleskin pouch from his pocket and set it on the table. "Take good care of this. It isn't much money but it will feed you until you reach Glasgow."

Jamie listened silently. He was beginning to feel afraid as the time to leave grew nearer, but he wasn't going to disgrace himself by showing it.

"Do you want me to do anything here before I go?" he croaked, hoping his voice wouldn't break.

"You can stay by the fire for awhile, but don't fall asleep. Go to Gaston's house before dawn and see that you don't wake the village trying to get in."

"Duncan!" Andrew Cameron was halfway out the door in his impatience.

"Keep that rattling tongue of yours under lock and key, Jamie," his father cautioned, "else it will hang you. We'll meet in Glasgow in the spring. Ask your uncle to teach you the tobacco trade. It will stand you in good stead in Virginia. Always remember that you bear the proud name of Macpherson, chief among the clan of the Cats! And guard this for me until I return."

A hug, a swirl of cloaks, a blast of icy air, and he was gone. Jamie stood alone in the room. He listened intently until the last hoof beat had died away. Then he looked down and saw that his father had thrust his snuffbox into his hand. Slowly he opened the tortoiseshell lid and gazed at the miniature painted inside it. The picture was of his mother.

She smiled up at him, her green eyes mischievous

beneath a mass of blazing red hair. Jamie's own eyes misted and he could see no more.

He dashed away the tears, angry at himself for this snivelling start to his adventure. Then he made a final inspection of the house. Had he forgotten anything?

Yes. The carved backgammon board lay on one side of the table, the pieces piled beside it. It seemed a long time since the last game. He folded the board, admiring the ingenuity with which it became small enough to stow away in his pack. Then he sat staring drowsily into the fire. He thought about Sleat, this stranger who wanted to kill him. "But I forgot to ask what he looked like!"

The enemy without a face floated in his head as he fell asleep.

2

Separate Paths

January 1759

"Sleat!" Jamie woke with the name echoing in his head. He rolled up his plaid, stuffed it into the top of his pack, and stumbled across the dark room. The logs that had crackled so cheerfully last night were now ashes, the air was brittle with cold. Cautiously, he opened the door and looked up and down the empty street. Gaston's house, across the way, was a silhouette, the timbered walls black against the snow in the dawn. He was about to close the door and run over when he stared again at the glistening carpet of snow. "I might as well paint signs on the walls to show them where I've gone, if I walk on that."

He thought for a moment, then walked to the wood pile and back to the cottage—four times to make a well trodden path—on the fifth trip he climbed over the pile and crawled through the bushes. He stayed well away from the road until he was a safe distance from the cottage and then darted across. By the time he reached Gaston's house he was sweating despite the freezing air.

He pushed the door, but it was bolted. He knocked lightly, but no one came. The rising sun sent long shadows across the snow, and a seagull shrieked in the distance. Jamie decided to hide in the shed until Gaston awoke. The shed door creaked on its hinges but nothing stirred.

He fumbled his way inside and found a corner out of the drafts that whistled through the cracks. He unrolled his plaid, covered his feet with a bundle of straw and settled down to wait.

"I hope Gaston rises early today."

He heard another sound in the wind. Horses! He peered through a knothole in the wall of the shed. Black-cloaked figures were dismounting, moving into position, surrounding his cottage across the street. Two disappeared behind the house, two stood by the side, and two at the door. A seventh figure remained on horseback surveying the scene. All were now motionless.

"Like birds of prey," whispered a voice in Jamie's ear. He started violently, then saw it was Gaston who stood beside him, peering through another hole in the wall.

They both watched silently. At a signal from the hooded figure on horseback the two men broke down the door and disappeared inside the cottage.

"Time for us to go while they are busy." Gaston opened the shed door and moved quickly across to his house. He went inside and signalled to Jamie who was so intent on walking in Gaston's footprints in the snow that he tripped on the doorstep and fell into the kitchen.

"Always good to make an early start to the day," Gaston beamed down at him. "I see your father had to leave before his visitors arrived. They will be very disappointed!"

This was a long speech for Gaston who seldom said much but was good at listening. As a result he knew more than anyone in the village. Jamie's father trusted him completely.

He started to repeat his father's message and to describe what had happened, but Gaston stopped him. It seemed that he had already heard.

"Don't worry. We'll have you on your way to Scotland on the next tide. But we'll have some breakfast first. Marie?"

Madame Leblanc came bustling into the kitchen. "Well, you old goat," she said, picking up a ladle and shaking it at Gaston. "Have you decided to mend your ways or do you want to spend tonight in the shed as well? I heard you scratching at the door at dawn. You are lucky that I am a gentle, forgiving woman, or I would not have unbolted it for a week."

As she swung around the table, still brandishing the ladle, she almost fell over Jamie. "Heavens, child. What are you doing on my kitchen floor at this hour?"

Gaston pointed to the window to the men coming out of the cottage, gathering around the motionless figure on horseback.

Madame Leblanc looked at her husband. "So they have come."

He nodded. She frowned, then reached down and pulled Jamie to his feet. "Sit and eat." She tore off the end of a loaf of bread and handed it to him. "You won't get cheese like this in Scotland," she said, passing him the plate. "But maybe when you're a rich merchant you'll make some trade with the Leblancs."

Gaston helped himself, too. "While we eat, Marie will think of how to smuggle you on board without your visitors getting in the way."

Jamie ate hungrily, all the while expecting a knock at the door. Just as he finished, Madame Leblanc appeared, beaming, with an armload of clothes.

"Here. These are Gilles' old breeches. They don't fit him any more, but they'll fit you, and they'll keep out the cold better than what you have now. Put them on and this shirt and sweater, and his old coat. Then pack your own."

When he had done this she inspected him from head to foot, then gave a small sniff of satisfaction. "With Gilles' cap even Grandmère would think he was Gilles—except for that red mop of his." She turned to her husband. "How do we give him Gilles' black hair?"

Silently, Gaston reached into the chimney—and scooped out a handful of soot. "Black you asked for and black you get," he said, rubbing Jamie's head vigorously. They both roared with laughter as his pale face peered out from beneath soot-black hair.

"It won't last forever but it will do the job for now."

Madame Leblanc explained her plan. "Gilles expected

to sail on the morning tide and slept on board last night. But no one in the village knows this. All we have to do is to walk you down to the ship as Gilles and let you carry supplies aboard. When it's time to cast off, Gilles will come ashore and go home. That way no boy leaves the village."

"Can you walk like Gilles?" With that, Gaston picked up Jamie's pack, threw open the door and stepped out into the morning.

"Please let it work," Jamie prayed silently. He waved goodbye to Madam Leblanc, still chuckling over her own cleverness as she cleared away the breakfast things, and started after Gaston with what he hoped looked like Gilles' lop-sided swagger.

The village was no longer empty. It was beginning to stir with men and boys on their way to the jetty to load the fishing boats and catch the tide. The strangers stood in the middle of the road, stopping and questioning the men, and looking hard at the boys. They halted the priest on his way to the church and pointed to the abandoned cottage. Jamie saw him shrug and shake his head.

Then Jamie saw Sleat. It had to be him. A tall, thin man in a black cloak standing off to the side. Watching. Every so often one of the men would take off a boy's cap and look at Sleat. He would glance over briefly, then shake his head and the boy would be allowed to pass.

Jamie's knees almost buckled as he came closer. He could feel the sweat trickling down his back.

"Do they know what I look like?" he whispered.

"All they can know about you is that you resemble

your mother and that you have red hair. But if you want to fool them you will have to get that worried expression off your face. Come, my child. Try to look curious instead of like a hunted rabbit. It isn't every day we have this kind of excitement in the village."

They reached the first of Sleat's men. "What's all the fuss this morning?" Gaston asked.

"No fuss, mate," said the man, rubbing his hands to stay warm. "The gentleman over there is looking for his long lost nephew. He's a bit strange but harmless-like. We do it to humour him." He took Jamie by the arm and reached for his cap.

"Wait!" There was a screech from the road above, and everyone looked back to see Madam Leblanc charging down the hill as fast as her short legs could carry her, waving a broom.

"Hold onto the young devil," she cried. "I'll teach him to sneak off with his father without doing his chores."

The people scattered hastily to let her through.

"Run, Gilles," shouted Gaston and pulled Jamie out of the frozen grip of Sleat's man. Jamie ran and the crowd started to laugh as Madame Leblanc swung her broom in a fury at the air.

She turned on Gaston. "You get down there after that young villain and bring him right back to me or you'll starve for a month."

Gaston shuffled off after Jamie, protesting his innocence, while Madame Leblanc puffed her way back up the hill, and Sleat's men returned to the business of making sure that Jamie did not escape by boat.

Jamie didn't stop until he reached the shore. The round pebbles, smoothed and polished for centuries by the battering sea, scrunched beneath his feet. He sat on the jetty, panting clouds of steam, and waiting for Gaston to catch up with him. At least if Sleat's men were here, his father and Andrew Cameron must be safely on their way to Paris.

"Well, my child, wasn't she wonderful?" Gaston joined him, wheezing and chuckling. "They say a man is only as clever as his wife, and I'm the cleverest man in all Normandy. We'd better get you aboard now, before they decide to take another look at you."

The tide was almost in; most of the fishing fleet was fully afloat. Jean Leblanc rowed the dinghy over from their boat to pick up the last of the supplies.

"What's happening in the village?" he asked.

"Take the boy on board. Tell your father to see him safely to Scotland. He knows what is to be done. Duncan had to leave suddenly as we expected. Send Jacques below when you get on board, and then bring Gilles back to shore." Gaston's face grew suddenly stern. "Don't let them both on deck at the same time."

Jamie climbed into the dinghy and Gaston handed him his pack.

"Good luck, Jacques. Don't forget, we'll do some trading some day." He paused, rummaged in his pockets and produced a handful of coins. He inspected them closely and gave several to Jamie. "Scots coins," he explained. "Not much, but they'll buy you lodging."

"Thank you, Monsieur Leblanc," said Jamie. "Please

thank Madame Leblanc for everything." He grinned at the memory of her cavalry charge down the hill. "Ask her not to be too hard on Gilles for escaping his chores."

They soon reached the ship and climbed aboard. The captain, a thinner, spryer version of Gaston, was almost ready to sail. Jamie scarcely knew him because he spent most of his time on long voyages. Gaston always said that his brother was fishing on the Grand Banks of Newfoundland, but Jamie knew from Gilles' boasts that he was a smuggler who sailed even in the winter's worst storms.

"Are you bringing me another Gilles?" he asked his son as they came aboard. "One is more than enough."

"A change of plans, Father," said Jean and he quickly gave the message.

"Go below, Jacques. Tell Gilles what he has to do, but be quick about it," said the captain.

Gilles was doubly disappointed when he heard the story. "I lose my best friend and my first real voyage on the same day," he complained, "and on top of that my mother is waiting for me with a broom. Good luck, Jacques. Maybe I'll see you on my next voyage."

"I'd like you to have this to remind you of good times," Jamie stammered. He handed Gilles his pocketknife.

Gilles' dark eyes lit up, and then he looked sad. "This time you might need it."

"I have my dirk."

"I'd like to give you something," said Gilles, hunting through his pockets, "but I don't have anything here."

"I already have most of your clothes so I won't be forgetting you on the cold Scottish nights."

Suddenly embarrassed, the two boys were silent. Then, with a smile and a wave, Gilles climbed on deck. Jamie went up after he had gone, but mindful of Gaston's warning he kept well down out of sight of any watchful eyes on the shore.

As soon as the dinghy had returned, they hoisted the sail and headed for the open sea. Jamie watched the white cliffs of Normandy fade and, with it, the seven black-cloaked figures standing on the jetty. "I wonder if they know I've escaped?"

He saw the captain looking at the clouds and heard him say, "I don't like the look of that Judas sky." Jamie didn't know what he meant but it sounded ominous. He went below to find a space where he could stow his gear and take shelter from whatever the Judas sky might hurl at him.

"He knew we were coming." Sleat looked slowly from face to face. Each in turn protested, "Not me, sir."

"Someone knows my plans too well, or someone here talks too much." Sleat spoke in the slow, patient way that chilled his audience. He turned to the youngest of the group, a scrawny youth with the nervous grin of a jackal. "Tell me again what the poacher said."

"He'd been out all night, and before dawn he saw Macpherson and a stranger riding through the woods."

"He didn't see the boy, and he didn't know where they were heading?" asked Sleat.

The youth shrugged. "There was no boy."

"Then the boy must still be here," said Sleat, frowning. "But that

doesn't make sense. Duncan has never left the boy before. He knows that if he's here, we will stay until we find him. Is that what he wants? Does he want me to stay here looking for a red-headed boy who has vanished into thin air? Answer me, Sinn. What do I pay you for?"

Sinn looked up. He seemed an unlikely member of this gang of cutthroats. His face was hollow and worn like that of an old statue, and his white hair blew in all directions with the wind.

"The boy has sailed away," he said in a sing-song voice.

"We watched every ship and every boy. Only one boy went on board and he came back before it sailed," said Sleat. "Besides, he had black hair. We made sure of that when he came ashore."

"One boy goes on and one boy comes off. One bee flies into the hive and one bee flies out. Is it the same bee?" Sinn rocked back and forth in silent laughter. Then he reached down, scooped up a hand-ful of black mud, and smeared it on his white hair. "Will you pay me more if I grow young again?"

Sleat glared at him. "Someday I'll turn your white hair red—with blood. How long will it be before that fishing boat returns with its catch?"

"That boat had its catch before it left. Remember how low in the water it sat? He's away with the smugglers. If I were Duncan Macpherson, I'd say the boy was old enough to visit his uncle Archie." Sinn slid behind the others before Sleat could carry out his threat.

The Sooty Devil

January 1759

For a time the ship ran ahead of the storm. Jamie helped
to batten down the hatches, and then just before it struck,
Jean sent him to the hatch above the companionway that
led down to the galley. "Get below and don't let the sea
in after you," he shouted above the howls of the wind.

Jamie had never seen the sea in such a fury. The sails
strained to hold the wind, the mast shivered and groaned.
A wave rose above him, higher than a house, then crashed
down on his head. He held onto the hatch like a drowning man, while the water tried to scrape him off the deck.
He wrestled open the hatch, scrambled below and struggled to pull it closed, but it was jammed. Another wave
pounded the deck, drenching him again, and the freezing water poured through the hatch. The boat pitched

violently and the hatch slammed shut. Jamie fell the rest of the way down the ladder to the lower deck. As he lay gasping like a landed fish, his eyes became accustomed to the dark, and he saw Gilles' cousin Henri, wedged in the corner, calmly peeling onions for dinner.

"Well, Jacques," said Henri, who had many duties, including being the cook. "At least it's good weather for smugglers. Here, make yourself useful," and he threw him an onion.

The storm lasted two days, blowing them far off course. Then the wind changed in their favour and the ship slid easily and steadily through the water. "If this weather holds we'll have you in Scotland in no time," said Jean. "But first we have to try to make a sailor out of you."

Jean inspected the ship for damage from the storm. When he found a broken fitting or a rip in a sail, he would show Jamie how to fix it and then leave him to finish. Afterwards he inspected the work. A nod meant that it was well done. A swipe with a rope's end would remind Jamie that there was only one way to do a job on a Leblanc ship. He resented the blows until he remembered the storm they had survived and realised that if the sea found his mistakes, the penalty would be much harsher.

Jamie lost track of the days. Despite the constant dampness and the freezing spray, he was enjoying his new seafaring life. Late one afternoon Jean announced that they would soon be putting him ashore.

He stared into the fog that blanketed the ship. "How can you tell?"

"I can't," said Jean. "My father told me. I don't know how he knows but he's always right. He says that I'll be able to tell someday, and then I can be captain of my own ship. You should get ready. When we reach shore we don't waste time waiting for the excisemen to arrive. Have you money for food?"

"Yes. My father and Gaston gave me enough to get to Glasgow."

"Where is it?"

"Here, in my pouch," answered Jamie, reaching into his pack. He suddenly began to rummage around, his face ashen. "It's gone. It's been stolen!"

"That's your last lesson for this trip," said Jean, with a grin. "Here's your money. I took it when you first came on board. Next time it won't be a friend who robs you."

After Jamie recovered, Jean showed him how to sew most of his coins into his coat, and gave him a belt with a split lining in which to hide the rest. "Never show more than you need to buy your food, and sleep in your coat." He frowned.

"What stupid thing have I done now?" Jamie wondered.

"The sea has washed all the black out of your hair. Go to the galley and get more soot from the stove. There are spies and informers everywhere, and your enemies may have put the word out to watch for a boy with red hair landing from a French ship. Once you get away from the coast there will be plenty of other boys and redheads to confuse your enemies."

"We left Sleat in Normandy. You seem to expect him

to be waiting for me on the shore," said Jamie.

"There are faster ways back to Scotland than the one we took," Jean answered.

Jamie remembered the seven black-cloaked figures on the jetty in Normandy. "They won't be there," he told himself. He hoped.

He had his hair re-sooted and said goodbye to Henri, who gave him two onions and a lump of cheese. As he climbed back up on deck, he could hear the dull roar of waves breaking on the shore, somewhere out there in the fog.

The anchor was lowered silently into the water and almost immediately a rowboat appeared alongside.

"A fine night for the fishing, Captain Leblanc," called a voice from below. A stubby man in oilskins and high boots clambered on deck.

"Rob, you old villain. I thought you were in prison," answered the captain. "Welcome." To Jean he said, "Get the cargo and the boy ashore as fast as you can. Tell me as soon as you're ready to sail."

Jamie went ashore with the third boatload of goods. He carried a cask through the shallow water to the beach, trying not to slip on the seaweed-covered rocks, following the line of shadowy figures who were unloading the bales and barrels from the rowboat as soon as it reached the shore. He dumped the cask with the others beside a row of shaggy ponies and kept walking, away from the sea. It was a strange feeling to be on solid ground again. As the land began to rise, he found a path which led him to the top of the cliff overlooking the smugglers' bay. No one had challenged him, and he finally allowed himself a sigh of relief.

It was a clear, moonless night on the cliff top. "Now I have to get away from the coast as fast as possible and head west toward Glasgow." He repeated Gaston's instructions, took his bearings from the stars and, swinging his pack over his shoulder, strode briskly across the moorland.

By the time the sun rose, he had walked several miles and felt that he had his land legs back again. He also felt hungry. He reached a track which seemed to be leading in a westerly direction and decided that he was far enough from the sea to pass himself off as a wandering country boy heading for the town. Captain Leblanc had told him that he spoke English well, but that the Scots brogue he'd learned from his father had French sounds mixed in with it. "Some people will hear Jacobite in that tongue of yours, so you'd better use it sparingly," he'd cautioned.

After another mile Jamie saw a farmhouse set among a stand of trees. "I should beg for bread," he thought. "That would be less suspicious than trying to buy it."

A short square woman stood over a washtub at the side of the house, jabbing the clothes with a stick and singing loudly. "Please, ma'am, could you spare a piece of bread?"

She stopped singing and stared at him silently. Then she looked toward the open door of the house. He followed her gaze and saw two loaves of bread and a pile of oatcakes on the table. She motioned for him to come closer.

When he reached her, she yanked the stick out of the tub and tried to grab him, but Jean's warnings had made him wary. He ducked and ran, and she screeched after him, "You young rascal. You want to steal my oatcakes."

Jamie stopped behind a hedge when he saw that she was not chasing him. "What a friendly place," he muttered.

He watched her from his hiding place. Now she was beating the clothes in the washtub as though they were him. He decided to teach her a lesson and crept around to the back of the house. He pushed open a small window and climbed silently inside. Careful to keep away from the open door, he edged around the wall. Then he reached over and grabbed a loaf. Just as his fingers closed around the warm bread, another hand seized the back of his neck.

"Got you," the woman shouted triumphantly. "I knew you'd come back. Your kind always do." She dragged him out of the house as if he were a bag of laundry.

Jamie's feet thumped the ground every third step as he was frog-marched to the washtub. She plunged his head into the tub and yanked it up and down under the water until he was sure he would drown. He could hear her screaming at him but the words were muffled and far away.

"You black-haired rogue, I'll teach you not to steal." She pulled his head out of the tub. Then she screamed again and let him go. "Devil!" she cried, and ran into the house slamming the door behind her.

Jamie stood, spluttering wash water, with his clean hair

sticking out in all directions. Flaming in the morning sun. When he realized he was free, he ran first to the bushes to pick up his pack and then down the road as fast as he could stagger. He went about half a mile before he felt that it was safe enough to stop. Only then did he notice that he was still clutching the bread.

"Almost drowned in a washtub after surviving a storm at sea. A fine adventurer I am," he said as he settled down under a tree by the roadside. "I wonder what gave her such a fright?"

He ate half the loaf with a piece of the cheese that Henri had given him for the journey, and stowed the rest away in his pack. He was tired from being up all night but thought it best to put as many miles as possible between himself and the coast. Clouds covered the low winter sun and rain began to drizzle as he set off again. Late that afternoon, Jamie came to a stone bridge over a fast-flowing stream. The brown water splashed and foamed as it rushed between the rocks. The road split on the other side of the bridge, giving him the choice of going downstream and north, or upstream toward the hills. He didn't want to travel north, but he was worried about getting too far into the hills on a cold winter night.

He put his pack down and sat on the bridge, listening to the water. He began to drop twigs into the stream, watching them disappear under the arches. An old man came shuffling down the road from the south with an ancient dog trailing at his heels. He stopped beside Jamie on the bridge and dropped a twig into the water himself. "I always enjoyed doing that when I was a boy," he said and started to walk on. After his experience with the woman, Jamie was a little shy of strangers, but the old man seemed harmless. "Will I reach the next village before dark if I take this road?"

"If you step lively, you will."

"Does the road lead to Edinburgh?" asked Jamie, encouraged.

"Why would you go to Edinburgh?" the old man snapped. "That's not a fit place for a God-fearing boy to go to."

Jamie was surprised and found himself explaining that he only wanted to go to Edinburgh in order to pass through on his way to Glasgow. This was more than he had planned to tell a stranger.

"That's different," said the old man warmly. "I can understand you wanting to go to Glasgow. I was born in Glasgow, but that has nothing to do with my opinion of the place you understand."

Jamie nodded. "The road," he prompted.

"Ah yes, the road will lead you to Edinburgh through the low hills. The other road will lead you there by the coast. But take my advice and give the place a wide berth. There's nothing but pride and poverty in that town. What's your hurry, anyway? You look a bit tired. Why don't you rest the night and start afresh in the morning? You can sleep on the floor by the fire with Rory here," he said, pointing his stick at the old dog that was sniffing at Jamie's pack and wagging its feathery tail. "You can do a bit of work for the price of your lodging, if you like."

Jamie accepted the offer gratefully. He followed the

old man along the road to a small cottage. On the way Jamie gathered dead wood and kindling for the fire. They made a meal by sharing the old man's soup and the remains of the bread and cheese.

When Jamie awoke in the morning, a pot of porridge was bubbling on the fire. "It's a good day to be on the road," said the old man, coming into the house. "You must have been worried about the weather. You muttered 'sleet' several times in your sleep. We may get a sleet storm soon but it won't be today."

The name brought Jamie awake as it had done on his last day in Normandy. "I hope I don't talk in my sleep very often," he thought.

He made good time that day and by nightfall was just east of Edinburgh. He found a handful of frostbitten leeks and a turnip for his dinner, and that night he slept under a hedge. The next day, skirting south of the town, he picked up the Glasgow road on the west side. There were more travellers on this road, more villages to pass through, more coaches and carts to add interest to the journey. He felt safer now, even though some of the groups he met looked as if they would rob their own grandmothers. Covered in the dust of travel, his worn clothes gave him safe passport among the wanderers. He was passed by milkmaids riding to town with barrels of buttermilk strapped across their donkeys, and red-coated soldiers patrolling the countryside. Once a battered wagon hung with pots and pans jangled by.

The man with the reins shouted words which Jamie couldn't understand, and the group of children peering at him from the back of the wagon laughed.

Early in the morning of the fourth day, Jamie sat in the shelter of a rock by the roadside trying not to think about how hungry he was.

"Be ye going to Glasgow?"

Jamie sat up. A plump white horse pulling a small cart had pulled up beside him. It was driven by an equally plump old man with a white fluff of hair encircling his gleaming pink head.

"Be ye a footpad?"

The old man leaned forward and inspected him closely from head to muddy foot, then turned and addressed the empty seat beside him. "William, do you think he be a footpad?"

"No?" He seemed satisfied by the reply from his invisible companion.

"Climb up then," he said. "You come up here beside me and William will move back."

Jamie was unsure about travelling with this man who talked to the air, but he seemed kindly, and Jamie was tired.

"Where be ye going?"

"The Trongate," Jamie said cautiously.

"The Trongate! Him be getting above himself," said the talkative old man with deep disapproval. "That's where the nobs live. You don't want to have anything to do with that lot.

"What do you think of that, William?" he shouted to the back of the empty cart.

"No good comes of associating with nobs. That's what

William says."

He looked at Jamie's dust-caked face and laughed. "But that doesn't seem much of a danger for you at the moment."

Jamie laughed too, a little uncertainly, and the cart bumped along.

At noon they stopped at an alehouse where the old man insisted on treating him to a large bowl of broth and a bannock.

"I was thinking," he said, as he watched Jamie scouring the last of the broth from the bowl, "that you wouldn't say no to a currant bun."

While the old man smoked his pipe, Jamie finished the best meal he had ever eaten. After the old man paid the bill, they returned to the cart and the fat white pony clopped off once more.

Jamie plucked up courage to ask the question which had been on his mind since they met.

"Please excuse me if this is a rude question. I don't mean to offend you, but why do you talk to someone called William who isn't here?"

The old man chuckled. "I do it so often now that I forget it seems strange to others. For years my brother and I were partners. We travelled everywhere together and I would prattle on to him about whatever was on my mind. When he died a year ago I was very lonely. There was no one to talk to on my long journeys, no one to share a joke or have an argument with. I gave up the business for a while, but that made matters even worse. Then one day I remembered that in all our years of travelling together, I had come to know how William looked at things and what he would say. And what William said was never very much at any time. We had an ideal partnership. I started travelling again, and William travels with me in spirit. Sometimes I even think I can hear him laughing at a joke. Now wouldn't that add something to life in heaven if you could hear the odd joke? Some people say James Wallace is a strange one, but I just go about my business.

"And here we be," he said, encouraging the pony with promises of oats. "The most beautiful city in Scotland."

Jamie stared in wonder as they approached the fairest city he'd ever seen: a forest of towers and spires arose in the distance. They drove through fields and orchards, leafless now in the cold. A church steeple soared high on a hill, sharp-etched against the winter sky.

The old man proudly pointed out the sights of the town. "There be the High Kirk and Fir Park beside it."

That was the tall slender spire that he'd seen from the outskirts of the city.

They drove through fine broad streets and along the Trongate past the Tolbooth. "The prison," Wallace said darkly. "I'll let you off here. The nobs live down that way, and if you go poking about down there you may end up back here," he said, nodding toward the prison. The town is a fair place during the day, but it gets rough in some quarters at night. Go down that alley until you come to David Blackadder's smiddy. He's an old friend of mine. He'll help you find a place to spend the night." With a wave he rattled off toward the bridge.

Jamie saw that he was talking to William as he went.

4
Free Passage
February 1759

Jamie watched the little cart drive off down the busy street. He'd like to have stayed with the old man and his invisible brother, but he knew that he should find his uncle.

He listened to the clatter and stared at the crowds that seemed to flit like sparrows in all directions at once. He had never seen so many people.

"Catching flies, are you?"

The voice startled him. A small girl in a large blue bonnet looked up at him. She switched her basket from one arm to the other and repeated her question.

"No," he answered in confusion.

"Then you'd best close your mouth." She whisked off down an alley with a flourish of skirts.

He picked up his pack and caught up with her. "Excuse me," he said. "Since you enjoyed teasing me, maybe you wouldn't mind helping me. I'm looking for David Blackadder's smiddy."

"After me then," she said and ran on.

Jamie followed, until he had to squeeze against the wall of a building to let a horse and cart go by. He lost sight of her, but within a few yards found her talking to a big man with a curly black beard and a leather apron. The smithy ran his fingers through his beard as he listened and sweat trickled down his soot-streaked chest.

"This is the boy who is looking for you, Father," she said as Jamie arrived.

"I've no work for you, if that's what you want."

"No sir, at least not yet." Jamie was determined not to show his surprise in front of the girl. "Mr. Wallace said that you would tell me where to spend the night. He seemed to think that if I wandered the streets I might not see the morning."

David Blackadder smiled. "He may be right, but if I take in every stray cat in town, I won't have room to stand in the smiddy. Why have you come to Glasgow?"

He saw Jamie's hesitation. "Tell me or not, as you wish, but don't tell me lies. I can't stand liars or thieves. You can spend the night by the forge. That will keep you from freezing to death."

Jamie blushed under the dust on his face. "This will sound like a lie, but I have to give a message to a man called Archibald Gilchrist."

"*The* Mr. Gilchrist?"

Jamie nodded and looked down at his bedraggled clothes.

"That's so unlikely that it has to be true," said the girl.

"My father told me to look for Willie the Ferret, if I couldn't find Mr. Gilchrist."

"That would be easier," said the blacksmith. "And what news do you bring Willie from France? Och, don't be afraid," he added when Jamie looked ready to bolt back down the alley. "I just thought from the cut of your cap, and the sound of your words, that you might be from France. I'm not going to call for the redcoats."

Jamie took his cap off and his hair sprang out of captivity. "It was supposed to hide my hair," he said ruefully, "but it won't do much good here if everyone knows it's French. Some men—enemies—may be looking for me. I keep putting soot on my head but it has a way of getting washed off."

"We have plenty of soot for you here," said the girl.

"Leave your pack in the corner," said the blacksmith. "It will be quite safe. Janet will take you on a tour of the town as her cousin from Ayr, and at six o'clock we'll try to help you find Willie. But you'd better clean yourself up a bit if you're to escort that fine young lady," he said, pointing into the smiddy at a trough of water.

When Jamie emerged he had washed and beaten the dust out of his coat.

The blacksmith watched them start along the alley. Then he called his daughter back and gave her a coin.

"Buy him a cap," he said. "I knew the Gilchrists a long time ago, and he reminds me of someone. He may remind others with all that red hair flying in the wind."

"What's your name?" Janet asked as they walked out of the alley. "I have to call you something if I'm to take you around the town. But I confess I like all the mystery."

"Jamie."

"Jamie who?"

"Jamie Blackadder if I'm your cousin," he replied, dodging the kick she aimed at his ankle.

They strolled through the streets past women with baskets of vegetables on their backs, and others carrying loads of sand—to clean the stone floors and steps—Janet told him. There were brushmakers and carts loaded with peat and coal. A small boy cried "toasting forks," at the top of his lungs, and a carter strode by with a barrel of herring on his shoulder. They climbed up to the cathedral and wandered among the dark firs on the hill in the park behind it. Finally, when they came back down to the Tolbooth again, Jamie asked if he could see where Archibald Gilchrist lived.

"We're nearly there." Janet led him past a wall of massive stone houses jutting out over columned arcades. "He lives at the end of this row. Grand place, isn't it?"

Jamie, trying not to be overawed by its sombre magnificence, looked up at the gables and the dormer windows glinting in the late afternoon sun, and then, thoughtfully, at the people scurrying by. They were delivering goods or going home to their suppers. Except for...

He stopped and bent down. "Just a minute, I have a stone in my shoe." He took his time shaking the shoe and watched. He'd been right. Two figures in that hurly-burly of a crowd were not moving. One man stood in a door-way across from his uncle's house, smoking a pipe. The other leaned against a wall at the end of the street. As Jamie watched, the second man stretched and started to walk toward the first. Jamie lost sight of him among the crowd.

"They're watching the house," he said to Janet. "We should go back to the smiddy."

"I like this," she whispered. "Are you a spy? No, don't tell me, it will probably be a disappointment. When I tell my sister Meg about the excitement she missed today, she'll have a conniption."

Jamie pulled his new cap more securely over his hair, and they retreated through a tangle of alleyways.

"Just let them try to follow us now," Janet said with satisfaction.

As they entered the dark heat, the smiddy rang with hammer blows. David Blackadder was forging a horse-shoe in the glow of the fire, closely watched by a tall boy who seemed all bony arms and legs and elbows. The blacksmith plunged the iron into the trough of water and came over to them as it sizzled.

"Did you enjoy the town?"

"Mr. Gilchrist's house is being watched!" Janet exploded with her news.

Blackadder looked at Jamie. "Is this true or have you been encouraging Janet's overactive imagination?"

Jamie flushed. "I think I saw two men watching the house, but I can't be sure."

"Well Janet, watchers or not, it is time you were home.

Young Calum will take your friend to meet Willie. Maybe he can sort this out."

"Take care Jamie, and don't let them catch you," she called back as she left. "Just wait until I tell Meg about this. She'll be green with envy."

"She thinks I'm a spy," Jamie said to the blacksmith.

"For my sake I hope she's wrong. Calum will take you to The Black Bull. Willie usually goes there. Leave it to Calum to arrange a meeting. You'd better take your pack since we don't know where you'll go from there, but if you don't find shelter, you can come back here. Calum spends the night in the forge and he'll let you in."

The apprentice led the way through streets and alleys which only an hour ago had been crammed with cheerful people but were now almost empty—fogbound and sinister. Occasionally a torch threw a smoky light on the dripping side of an alley, but Jamie found this even more frightening than the darkness. In the shadows cast by the torches, the bystanders looked like assassins waiting for a victim. He was grateful for the company of the apprentice blacksmith, with his gap-toothed grin.

They reached The Black Bull. "Wait here by the door while I find Willie," said Calum and ducked inside. Jamie clutched his pack for the shelter it gave and watched the people stumbling by, huddled against the freezing wind. "Did Glasgow ever sleep?" he wondered.

Just when he felt that his fingers might drop off from the cold, he became conscious that someone was watching him. A thin figure in a long black coat came out of the shadows of the doorway opposite and walked slowly toward him. The light from the alehouse window cast a yellow glow onto his lined face and the wisps of hair that poked out from beneath his tall hat.

"Well, boy," he breathed in a soft voice. "I'm Willie. What do you want with me?"

"I don't know any Willie," stuttered Jamie. The man gripped him by the collar and with one hand lifted him into the light of the window. He took off Jamie's cap and held him there, turning him slowly one way and then the other, like a fish on a scale.

"A fine likeness," he murmured.

Jamie squirmed and wriggled, trying to break free, but it was useless. The old man's grip was like a vice. The alehouse door swung open splashing light on the road, and Calum came out. The man dropped Jamie and disappeared down an alley. Calum started after him and then stopped. "Are you all right?"

"Fine," said Jamie shakily. "Just scared to death."

He *might* have imagined the watchers outside his uncle's house that afternoon, but the face in the yellow light was real. Sleat's men were in Glasgow—and had found him.

Calum smiled. "You'll survive here, if you know enough to be frightened. Come on in and meet Willie."

Calum led him through a room filled with smoke and ale fumes and the noise of clashing plates and tankards. A woman, rosy and cheerful, forced her way through the crowd with glasses of ale for a group playing cards in one corner. Everywhere was noise and jostling, but it seemed good-natured. A band of Highlanders were standing at one end of the room singing a dirge. All the people from the street must have found their way here, Jamie decided. The noise, heat and light shocked him out of his fright. When they reached a table against the far wall, Calum motioned to him to slide into the bench first. He sat down and looked across. The little man bundled inside two coats was wrapped in a long black scarf and wore gloves without fingers. The candle on the table lit one side of his pale face. Jamie sat, unable to move. Hypnotized like a rabbit, just as Andrew Cameron had foretold. Willie's long fingers poked out from his gloves and wrapped themselves around a bowl of hot peas. The sharp smell of the vinegar wafted over to Jamie and made his eyes water. *A good friend and a bad enemy.* He remembered the warning and hoped for the best.

When Willie finally spoke, his voice was a surprise. It should have been thin like the rest of him, but it was hoarse, grating. "Like a man who's been hanged," Jamie thought.

"You want to meet Willie? Well here I am. You've eaten well today so I won't offer you any peas." He pushed the bowl over to Calum who took it eagerly and began to eat.

"A hungry boy would look at the food," he continued, "but you stare at me."

"Excuse me," Jamie apologized. "I didn't mean to stare. It's just that I've been trying to guess what you would look like."

Willie puffed on his pipe, and when Calum had finished the peas he told him to go back to the smiddy. "I have a few questions to ask the boy."

When Calum had left, with a friendly wave, Willie said abruptly, "take your cap off." Then he smiled, displaying blackened snaggle teeth. "Put it back on. You're the image of your mother. And how is that rogue Duncan Macpherson?"

"How did you know so easily? Does everyone in Scotland have second sight?"

"David Blackadder guessed. He told Calum to tell me that he was sending a small cat. David likes riddles. I thought of many cats but when I saw you I realised he meant Clan Chattan, someone from the clan of the Cats. Now I want to hear your story. But first, do you think anyone else knows you are here?"

Jamie described the men watching his uncle's house that afternoon and the wraith who called himself Willie. "He held me up to the light and stared at me with eyes that looked like the eyes of a blind man. He seemed to look through me, not at me." Jamie stopped and shivered, despite himself.

Willie frowned and tapped the table with his long fingers. "I know about the watchers. I've been wondering what they wanted. The man outside could only be Sinn. He works for Sleat. Did your father tell you about Sleat?" Jamie nodded and Willie went on, "Sinn is a strange one. He may have told Sleat already, or he may not. He works by his own rules. He does Sleat's bidding but only when it suits him, and he gets away with it because he is the only man on God's earth that Sleat trusts."

"He frightened me out of my wits," Jamie confessed.

"I'll wake up in the night with those pale eyes staring at me."

Willie laughed. It was a strange sound, like chains scraping together in a cellar. "You were lucky. I think he wanted to satisfy his curiosity that he had found the right boy. If he had it in mind to kill you or take you to Sleat, you wouldn't be here now. That's what I mean by working to his own rules.

"I remember a Highlander from Skye telling me that Sinn was like a great gannet hovering far above the earth, watching everything below with cold, all-seeing eyes and when the moment was right, diving for the kill with ruthless deadly force. The Skye man was escaping from Sinn on a boat bound for the Hebrides. Three weeks later they found him, drifting in a small boat with his skull crushed and a gannet with a broken neck draped over his body."

"But how?" croaked Jamie. More afraid than ever.

"No one knows, but the Skye man must have told others of his vision of Sinn as that great white seabird, and talk like this would reach Sinn. It would appeal to his sense of humour to find a way to give the story a fitting end."

Willie signalled to a boy to come to the table and whispered to him. The boy vanished into the crowd. A few minutes later he reappeared. Jamie couldn't understand what he said, but it was obvious from Willie's expression that the news was bad.

"They're waiting for us, right enough, but we're in no hurry. So I'll just have a drop of brandy while you take your time and tell me your story. They may get a bit stiff with the cold, and that could be useful to us. Besides, it's time I fed Fergie."

"Three pies and a brandy," he ordered.

When the boy came back, with three pies balanced in his hand, Willie gave one to Jamie and one to the boy. Then he reached inside his coats and produced a ferret. The little animal blinked its pink eyes in the light and began to nibble Willie's pie.

"Watch them," he said to the boy. "Tell me if they get restless." The boy nodded and still munching on his pie, left to work his way through the crowd, which was rapidly turning quarrelsome.

Jamie told Willie all he knew. How Andrew Cameron had visited on the night of his birthday, of his father's plan to meet in Virginia in the spring. After days of fending for himself, it was a relief to have someone he could trust to talk to. Willie listened intently, asked a few questions, and occasionally spoke to the ferret. Then he held open a pocket and Fergie disappeared inside as though going down a rabbit hole. From another pocket he produced a pen, paper and a small pot of ink and began to write rapidly.

"This is just a note to your uncle in case we get into difficulties."

"What if it falls into Sleat's hands?"

"Don't worry. Even if it did, it's in your uncle's business code. It wouldn't make any sense to anyone else. We'll go to the river. They won't expect that, and I'll send you to a friend in Partick where you'll be safe until your uncle can sort out what's to become of you."

The boy returned as Willie finished his note.

"Take this to Mr. Gilchrist in the morning if I'm not back." He wrapped his scarf around his neck and stood up. "Time for us to go now."

Willie pushed his way through what now looked like a rioting mob, to the back of the alehouse, and then down a flight of stone steps to the cellar. The owner, a pot-bellied bear of a man, nodded cheerfully as they went by. "Taking the quiet way, Willie?"

Jamie kept close behind as the passage became dark and narrow. The air was damp with the fumes of old ale and mould. They twisted and turned until he began to feel dizzy, then at last he could smell fresh air.

"The road to the river is just ahead," Willie whispered. "Wait here."

He was back in a moment. "Safe as houses. It's good to know that Sinn hasn't discovered all my secrets."

They soon reached the river. "This isn't the best place to be at this time of night, but we haven't much choice. About half a mile from here I can get a boat and we'll have you safe away."

They walked along the bank by the light of a half-moon and came upon a small group of people huddled around a fire. The gaunt, hopeless faces in the firelight turned, one by one, to watch them. Jamie stayed close to Willie and took a firm grip on his sleeve.

"It's all right. They are just poor wretches with no place to lay their heads. They won't harm you."

Jamie was reassured, but he was glad when no one from the fire followed them. Glasgow at night had changed its shape just as James Wallace had warned. He hadn't been afraid of the dark since he was small, but now the nameless dread of forgotten nightmares had come back.

Willie slowed down as they approached a single figure sitting beside a large warehouse.

"We may have to run here, Jamie. He's near as big as the building."

The figure spoke.

"Have you a bite to eat, friends? It's a long way I am from my home and I'm thinking I should have stayed there. I mean you no harm but a starving man gets desperate." Slowly, he unfolded his great frame and towered over them.

Jamie's fear disappeared. This was a Highlander. During their roving years, he had met many men like this, fellow exiles in France. He replied in Gaelic. "Is it to rob a boy that you left home, Highlander?"

The giant sat down and held his tousled head in his hands. "I am ashamed. Pay me no heed."

"Here," said Jamie, and he offered him the half-pie that he had saved from the alehouse.

The man's face was a confusion of hunger and pride.

Willie spoke softly. "We need a strong back to row us down river."

The Highlander took the pie and was on his feet in an instant, with a beam of relief on his face. "You are the first people to show kindness to Angus MacCrimmon since he left Skye. I will be rowing you to the ends of the earth if that be your wish."

"Not that far," said Willie, "but I like the sentiment."

They set off again into the murk. Angus picked up his pack and followed them.

"We're almost there," said Willie. "It's on the other side of the bridge."

They were halfway under the arches when the four men stepped out to block their way. Jamie looked back and saw three more in the path behind. "It's a trap!"

"There's only four of them," said Angus, looking ahead. He set his pack down gently and with a battle cry that echoed from the bridge overhead, he charged at the men in front of him. Willie saw what Jamie meant and turned to face the trio who ran toward them, raising their billy clubs as they came. The first to reach him swung his club in a vicious arc at Willie's head. Jamie shouted a warning, but when the club landed, Willie wasn't under it. At the last moment he had slid to one side. Now he struck and the man dropped with a scream of pain.

Jamie looked back. He saw Angus pick up the first man to reach him and throw him into the river. Then he felt a crushing pain in the back of his neck and the cold mud covering his face as he was smashed into the ground.

When he became conscious again, he found himself tied hand and foot, roped to Willie on one side and Angus on the other. Blood ran down Willie's face from a gash above his eye. Angus was still unconscious.

"Sleat." Jamie managed to spit the word out.

"These aren't Sleat's men," Willie smiled. But with one eye closed and blood dripping from his chin, it was not a pleasant sight. "You're about to join the King's navy. You wanted to go to Virginia, well, you're going to get a free passage. We've just been press-ganged."

It was morning and Sleat paced behind his desk in his warehouse. Five of his men stood uneasily in front of the desk. Sinn came into the room and stood by the window, looking down at the river, watching the patches of fog drift across the black water.

"The boy has disappeared again. You had him trapped in The Black Bull and you let him escape. Where is Willie?"

"Gone."

"Gone where?" demanded Sleat. "Sinn, damn you, stop gawking at the river and tell me where Willie could be."

"He's joined the navy," Sinn said quietly, without turning from the window. "Poor Willie. He thought he'd finished with the sea, and the navy's not his style. Willie's not fond of floggings."

"Stop drivelling on about poor Willie. How do you know this?"

"The widow Jarvie was fishing last night. She saw Willie and the boy taken by a press gang. She told Archie Gilchrist this morning. Such news earns a good dinner. You owe me the price of another."

Sleat threw him the money. Sinn caught it and returned to looking at the river.

"Where are they now?"

"Off to war in the land of ice," Sinn said in a tired voice.

"Don't give me riddles, you old villain. Where have they gone?"

"Canada," said Sinn. "First to Portsmouth and then to fight for King and country in that godforsaken wilderness. Poor Willie."

"Damn Willie," roared Sleat. "I want that boy. I want the cub to squeal until its father hears it. If we fail to catch him when he comes looking for the boy here, then I need to know where he will go next.

If we lose the boy we may lose his father forever."

Sinn started walking to the door.

"Where do you think you're going?" shouted Sleat.

"To send a raven to Portsmouth," said Sinn and closed the door quietly behind him.

5
The Loblolly Boy

February 1759

They reached Greenock in the morning and were herded aboard the receiving ship which was called *The Charming Betsy*.

"Her charms have faded long since," said Willie as they were taken over in the pressing-tender.

"Is this the ship we have to serve on?" asked Jamie, dismayed at the battered leaky hulk, wallowing in the water.

"No. She's just an old transport to take us south to Portsmouth. It will be a grim voyage, but the sooner started, the sooner over."

They climbed aboard and were marched across the deck to an open hatchway with steam rising into the cold morning air. Angus paused to look at the faraway hills across the steel-glinting water before climbing down into the hold after Willie.

Then it was Jamie's turn. He stared down into the black hole and gripped the rope. As he started to slide down, he breathed the dead air of the hold and the stench choked him. He panicked and tried to climb back up, but a sailor on deck put his foot on Jamie's head and shoved him down. Angus caught him at the bottom and Jamie clung to him like a drowning cat in a well.

"Just hang on. Willie will find us a place."

When Jamie's eyes adjusted to the dark he saw faces staring up at him from every part of the hold. Willie's voice cut through the clamour of shouts, moans and curses. "Bring him over here, Angus, and keep your head down."

Angus swung Jamie onto his back and crawled over the crowded bodies to reach Willie who was settled against the hull.

The hatch slammed shut, just as they squeezed into the space that he had claimed for them. Jamie huddled between the two men and stared blindly into the darkness. Someone began to scream. There was a thud and the screaming stopped. Jamie felt a clammy fear spread over him and began to shake.

"It's all right, lad," came Willie's rasp beside him. "It's only darkness. It can frighten you but it can't hurt you. Just hang onto Angus and me until the shakes go away. Tell Angus a story. Angus likes a story, don't you, Angus?

"Aye, Jamie," came the calm voice from the other side. "Tell us a story and help me forget this place."

Jamie didn't think that he knew any but he closed his eyes and the soft Gaelic words began to flow, telling the mournful tale of "Red Roderick of the Seals." Soon he stopped shaking and the fear crept out of his body.

For the next two weeks *The Charming Betsy* pitched and rolled through the Irish Sea with her stinking cargo. Jamie's fear came back many times but he now knew it would pass. He hated the rats that fought with the prisoners for the food that was flung down into the hold once a day. At first he was afraid to sleep because of them, but Willie let Fergie curl up with him and he felt protected.

"I should never have left Skye," mourned Angus for the hundredth time. "When I return, I will never be getting into a boat again, if I live to be a hundred."

"Well you're going to Canada now," said a voice in the darkness next to him. "We're off to help bloody Wolfe fight the bloody French, and we'll all be hacked to death by the bloody Indians." The thought seemed to give the voice grim satisfaction.

Jamie heard a splash and the rattle of the anchor chain.

"Portsmouth?" he asked.

"Very like," said Willie. "Now remember," he shook Angus to get his attention, "we stick together at all costs. Leave the talking to me."

"Look alive down there." A seaman slid the iron bar across the heavy wooden grating.

"Come on, Jamie," said Willie. "Angus, watch him at the top. The fresh air can make you dizzy after a spell below."

As he clambered on deck, the air hit Jamie like a blow

in the stomach and he staggered back, blinking in the sunlight. Angus held him up with one hand while he carried both their packs in the other.

"Over the side and into the boat," roared the sailor. "Shake a leg." He started to swing a knotted rope at Jamie, saw Angus looming behind and changed his mind.

"They'll take us before the Regulating Captain, then assign us to a ship," said Willie. "I've been through this rigmarole before. When we get there, stand up and look lively. If we can't get out of this, we must get aboard the best ship they have."

"If ever I am returning to Skye," Angus vowed again, "I'll not be leaving, no, should they make me chief piper to the Lord of the Isles."

The docks were swarming with people. Casks and barrels were piled everywhere. The last of the supplies were being loaded for the great expedition which was to leave for Quebec the next day. The street vendors were crying their wares. One man sang in praise of his sausages:

> They're round,
> They're very sound,
> They're naught but fourpence the pound.

Another offered, "Fine fresh water at a ha'penny a pail."

"Hurry it up," shouted the sailor who was herding them along.

A street musician played "The Press'd Man's Lamentation" as they straggled by, and Willie took up the song in his hoarse voice:

Now the bloody war's beginning,
Many thousands will be slain,
And it is more than ten to one
If any of us return again.

This revived the spirits of the bedraggled gang. Several of them joined in the chorus.

"In here, you flaming bunch of canaries," shouted their guard. They turned onto a narrow street near the docks outside a dingy alehouse called The Spotted Dog. An enormous flag flapped from a cobweb-shrouded window. With Angus close at his heels, still muttering dolefully about Skye, Jamie followed Willie into the alehouse, up the stairs and along a grimy hallway.

Through the open door, he could see a large room with pistols and cutlasses arranged on the wall behind a desk. An elderly officer in a crooked wig slumped, half-dozing, in a leather chair, with an aide yawning beside him.

"First," said the aide.

A small man scuttled forward, like an anxious crab.

"What are you?" asked the Regulating Captain.

The small man quivered and his ears turned pink.

"Spinks, the tailor, your worship."

"What brought you here?"

"That lieutenant and his gang took I in Greenock last month just as I were going home." Desperate, he gained courage and burst forth: "I shouldn't be here. I have a family to support. You can't press-gang an honest citizen."

"Can we not?" barked the Regulating Captain,

suddenly awake and threatening. "We want tailors on board as well as on shore, so you'll drive your needle there. Put him on the *Neptune*. They need sailmakers," he ordered. "Next."

Willie walked up to the table. "Sir, I work for Mr. Archibald Gilchrist of Glasgow, and these two boys are his wards."

"Boys?" interrupted the captain, squinting suspiciously at Angus.

"They are under age and I ask permission to take them back to Glasgow."

"There's a war on. Permission denied."

"Permission then requested to sail together, sir. I have experience at sea, and the boys are good workers."

"Step forward, misters." The officer looked closely at the threesome and nodded. "Send them all to Captain Everet's ship," he said to his aide. "Next."

They were taken outside, roped together, and turned over to a scowling sailor to be taken to the ship.

Jamie wasn't looking forward to more sea voyages, but he couldn't help enjoying the sights of Portsmouth. When they reached the high street, lined with inns and shops, they saw a colonel riding by at the head of a troop of Highlanders, their kilts swinging as they marched. The townspeople cheered and clapped, and a cluster of girls waved their handkerchiefs.

Groups of recruits fell in behind the regiment, closely followed by merchants brandishing bargains: gold watches for twenty shillings, gold wedding rings for fourpence. There were fiddlers and jugglers and pickpockets going quietly about their work. Three little boys offered to play "Britannia Rules the Waves" on their chins for a penny.

A chorus of noises rose from the dockyard in the distance: sawing and hammering, wood creaking, waves crashing on the shingle. Gunfire too, from the ships anchored off Spithead firing salutes.

And such ships they were. These were the mighty walls of oak of the British navy, their stubby hulls painted yellow and black with forests of masts looming above. Huge red ensigns flapped in the breeze. Gilded letters glittered in the sun, spelling out the names across the elaborately-carved sterns: *Neptune*, *Diana*, *Stirling Castle*.

As they were marched briskly across the docks Willie asked, "Is it a good ship or a floating hell?"

"The *Stirling Castle*, mate. One of the best."

"Then, how about sausages to celebrate?" Willie produced a coin from one of his pockets.

The sailor waved the sausage vendor over. "Don't let the lieutenant see you," he cautioned and they all munched away as he led them to the sally port.

Jamie went first. Then Willie inched his way down the slippery ladder and settled himself in the cutter that was to take them to their ship.

The rungs creaked alarmingly as Angus followed, sheltering his belongings from the bouncing waves.

"Feeling any better now?" Willie asked.

"That sausage was fit for a king, but I'm thinking I'm not going to like the navy." Angus's freckled face was tragic. "When will I be returning to Skye? My heart will break if I am not seeing my beloved land again."

"You'll survive, Highlander," said the sailor, who seemed in a better mood after his sausage. "We're taking boatloads of your cousins to fight the French in Quebec." He pointed to the transports that lay anchored in the distance. "You'll have company in your misery on the other side."

"Highland regiments in the fleet? I'll maybe be giving the old pipes a skirl," said Angus, brightening up immediately.

"Not yet, Angus. Not yet," pleaded Willie. "It's not everyone here is a great lover of the bagpipes."

The cutter set off, bucketing like a runaway horse in the waves. Jamie sniffed the salt spray, while regiments of gulls soared overhead. The air reminded him of Normandy. After the stench of the last two weeks, it was a pleasure just to breathe. They came closer and the shining hull loomed larger and taller before them.

"Willie," Jamie said quietly. "I can't fight against the French. All my friends are French. And how can I fight for the English? They killed my mother, and they'd like to hang my father."

"It's a strange life, Jamie. Many in the Highland regiments fought for Bonnie Prince Charlie at Culloden. Some were only children then, and suffered through the bloody aftermath of the war. They're here because their chiefs have deserted them for the soft life of Edinburgh, or because a man may gladly give his life in battle for clan honour, but to starve to death alone in the hills for a lost cause is another matter. You'll choose for yourself some day, but first we have to survive the Atlantic Ocean in the winter. That's enough to be getting on with the now."

"Here she is," the sailor said. "The *Stirling Castle*."

There was no more time to talk as they were shoved and heaved up the ship's side onto the quarterdeck. Slipping and sliding on the wet deck, they were quickly taken below, past barefoot sailors rolling casks of provisions, and dirty women lounging in corners with their sweethearts and mugs of beer, while the boatswain and his mates bellowed more loudly than the wind. They were brought to the black-whiskered purser, who issued bedding, a blue canvas shirt, a pair of baggy trousers, woollen stockings, and a red cap to each of them—except for Angus, who was too big to fit anything that the purser could find. "Wear your own shirt," he said, his whiskers twitching in despair. "I'll have to steal a sail to make one to fit you."

Then they were chivvied onto the lower gun deck—a long, shadowy, low-beamed place with a strong smell of tar.

"This will be home for a while," said the sailor, who seemed to be regaining his ill-temper. "You're in the navy now, misters. Set up them hammocks and stow your gear. One word of warning: don't try to go over the side. Some of the press'd men tries to escape before we leaves port, but no one gets away, and the punishment in war is death." He gave a farewell scowl and departed.

Jamie and Angus struggled unsuccessfully with their hammocks until they noticed that Willie was already rocking gently back and forth in his. When they threatened to tip him out on the deck he agreed to show them how to set theirs up.

"Do you know," said Angus, "when I was just a wee thing, my mother would warn me when I did something bad that I would be ending up in a dungeon in Stirling Castle."

"She didn't have second sight," said Willie, "but she came close."

The rest of the crew came off duty then and the room was suddenly full of sailors. They sat or sprawled at the mess tables, gulping beer and bellowing at each other in the stuffy darkness.

"I don't feel quite so much like a prisoner," said Jamie, when the bald man in the next hammock introduced himself as Shine, the Barber. He hospitably offered them "a chaw of tobacco" and began a lengthy description of how *he* had been press-ganged on the way to his wedding. "Just in the nick of time," he said cheerfully.

There was a sudden hush in the smoke-filled room. Jamie looked up and saw a man heading toward them followed by a small interested crowd. He was short and broad and swung his arms out from his body in a rolling swagger.

"I'm Wilson," he said, staring down at Willie, "and what I say goes on this deck. Understand?"

Willie looked him up and down as if memorizing every ugly feature. "I'm Willie, and this is Jamie and Angus. Lad, where are your manners? Stand up and say hello to the man."

Angus slowly unfolded from the floor where he had

been sitting, but he was far too tall to stand upright between the decks. He looked more massive than ever, crouched beneath the beam.

"I'd like to think we'll all get on just fine," Willie said. Somebody laughed. Wilson grunted and moved on.

The next day they sailed with the fleet for Canada and the hard work of manning the ship began. Jamie was glad he'd served his short apprenticeship with Jean Leblanc. He was able to help Angus escape the rope's end more than once by showing him what to do. Angus did not take kindly to scrubbing decks.

On the third day, when they were off-duty, he came to Willie in a fury. "Somebody has stolen my chanter. I thought I'd just play me a tune and it's gone. The MacCrimmons are pipers to kings. Nobody steals a MacCrimmon's pipes."

"Easy now, Angus," said Willie. "Let me try something before you go cracking skulls. Just you sit yourself down over by the bulkhead there. I'll be back in a minute."

Willie made his way slowly back to their mess table, talking casually to one or two of the men on his way. "A word with you." He summoned Jamie who sat swapping tall tales with another boy. "You wanted to give me that fine dirk of yours for safe keeping."

Jamie was puzzled but he had learned to trust Willie's strange ways, so he said, "Yes, it was my grandfather's," and handed it to him.

Willie held the dirk to the light of the porthole to

admire the carving, and felt the sharp steel with his thumb. Then he put it carefully in the pocket of the coat that lay on top of his gear in a corner.

Jamie went back to talk to his new friend, and Willie ambled over to Angus who sat muttering Gaelic curses.

"We'll just wait a bit and see if we catch us a fish." Willie settled down comfortably beside him. "Wake me if anything happens. Don't go near our gear unless I say so," and he nodded off to sleep.

An hour passed. Several of the sailors were asleep, but most were talking or playing cards, when a scream of agony came from the corner. Willie was up instantly. With Angus close at his heels, he rushed over in time to grab a blue shirt as it tried to reach the hatch. Willie couldn't hold him but Angus was there. He swung the sailor off his feet and threw him against the near bulkhead. Jamie brought a candle, and in its glow crouched Wilson, clutching his right hand. His face was twisted with pain.

"Well, thief," said Willie, "where's Angus's chanter and whatever else you've stolen?"

Wilson glared at him.

"I'll kill him," Angus said in a matter-of-fact way.

"No need to do that. Just look at his hand."

Wilson stared at his throbbing hand which had started to swell. Then his nerve broke. "It's up there." He pointed to the darkest corner of the beam overhead. Angus reached up to the crevice in the wood and gently removed the chanter.

"Now get the poison out of me," Wilson begged.

"Do you think I should try to do that?" Willie asked. "He'll probably die anyway."

Angus was too busy inspecting his chanter to answer, so Willie bent over the whimpering sailor. He made several cuts in the swollen hand with his knife. Then he rubbed it, sucked a mouthful of blood from the wounds and spat it out on the deck.

"Take him to the surgeon, Jamie. He'll do the rest." He turned back to Wilson. "One missing ha'penny on this deck and you'll be man overboard."

Jamie led a moaning Wilson down the companionway to the orlop deck where the surgeon had his cabin and knocked on the door.

"Come in."

The surgeon looked up from his book when they entered. He was a small, stubby man in a soup-spotted vest and a jacket so green with age that it looked mildewed. He had been eating onions and cheese as he read, and drinking brandy from a large cup made from a coconut shell. A candle guttered on the medicine chest beside him.

"I haven't seen you before, have I?"

"No, sir."

"Then who made you ill?"

The surgeon chuckled at Jamie's expression. "It's all right, my boy. Just an old medical joke. What's wrong with him? No, don't tell me, I can see the blood from here. Sit him down over there. Now fetch that bottle from the shelf. Yes, the one with the red top. Put a good dose on this cloth." He handed Jamie a rag and retreated to his chair on the other side of the cabin. From there he continued to give instructions. Wilson howled and thrashed about when Jamie washed the wound with the liquid from the bottle. "That's right, my boy. Well done. Now bind it up with the cloth."

"There you are," he said to Wilson. "Another life saved. Get back to your quarters until your next watch."

Wilson fled, and Jamie started after him. "Stop," cried the surgeon. "Come here, boy. What's your name?"

"Jamie Macpherson, sir."

"And I'm Surgeon Wackley. How d'ee do."

"Fine, sir." Jamie was becoming more confused by the moment.

"Jamie, you have the makings of a fine surgeon. I liked the way you handled all that blood. Can't stand the sight of blood myself. Always admired medical men who could stand the sight of blood. Not many of them can, you know." The surgeon produced a large snuffbox, took a pinch of snuff and continued talking in a succession of sneezes. "Here's how it is. My first mate is a drunken fool and my second mate is down with the jaundice and collicks, so I need an assistant. I think they call it a loblolly boy in the navy, but I'm not very strong on navy terms. How would you like the job? Take your time, think it over. The hours are good. The food is terrible but better than you get on the gun deck. The duties are simple, unless we get into a battle, God forbid. Well?" He stared at Jamie with shrewd brown eyes. "What d'you say?"

"Yes, sir."

"Splendid. Report in the morning."

When Jamie got back to his quarters, it was time to sleep. He told his friends about the surgeon and his new job.

"That's good news, lad," said Willie. "We expect a few scraps from the table, mind you. And while I remember, here's your dirk."

"Willie, was Wilson really poisoned?"

"No. He just got a fright, but don't tell a soul."

"What gave him such a fright?"

Willie opened his pocket and a small head looked out. "Fergie."

Sinn arrived late, while Sleat was haranguing the men.

"If you expect to catch Duncan Macpherson when he comes to Glasgow for his son, you will have to be more alert than you were when you let the boy escape. Is there no sign of Macpherson at all?"

"None," replied one of the men. "We have the Gilchrist house under watch day and night, and we have informers everywhere. If he arrives, we'll know."

"Well, Sinn," said Sleat, "what is taking him so long to get here?"

"He's been and gone," said Sinn. "It's not their fault they missed him," he went on when Sleat looked ready to explode. "He has the knack of doing the unexpected," he added with obvious respect.

Sleat stopped pacing behind the desk and sat down. When he became still like this, Sinn grew wary. There was a fine line between hate and madness, and when Sleat crossed it his rage was uncontrollable.

"When you are finished praising the rogue, would you mind telling me where you think he is now." Sleat leaned back in his chair

and eased his dagger from its sheath in his belt.

"He saw Archie and learned that the boy was on his way to Portsmouth. I would guess that Macpherson reached Portsmouth too late and that he will follow his son to Quebec."

"He can't just get on a ship to Quebec. The navy is commandeering every ship it can lay its hands on to carry soldiers and supplies to the war."

"To carry soldiers," repeated Sinn quietly. "Duncan would be a worthy recruit."

"How sure are you of this?"

"I'll know in a week.

"And there's another little matter I should tell you about," Sinn continued. "Archie Gilchrist arranged discharge papers for Willie and the boy and dispatched them to Portsmouth. Willie is no longer in the King's navy, but he doesn't know that yet. As soon as the papers reach the ship, the admiral will say how sorry he is to have inconvenienced Willie and wish him and the boy a safe journey home."

"I want these papers," hissed Sleat. "Intercept the messenger..."

Sinn reached into his pocket and threw a packet on the desk.

Sleat slid the papers into his pocket. "Now you are earning your keep. If Macpherson goes to Quebec, then we must go there too. Find out which of my ships is ready to sail and load it with provisions for the army. We will make it a profitable voyage in more ways than one."

6
Friend or Foe

April 1759

Life on board the *Stirling Castle* had settled into a hard routine of work, eat and sleep. Gun drill, which had been a hectic scene a few weeks ago, was now carried out with precision. This was due to Willie's talent for organizing the people around him. He had added Wilson to his own group. "It's easier to keep an eye on the scoundrel," he explained, and with Wilson and Angus he had the strongest and fastest gun crew on the ship.

Several of the marines were Highlanders. When they discovered that a MacCrimmon piper was on board, they asked permission for Angus to visit them and he would play reels while they danced on deck. He grew another six inches it seemed, out of pleasure and honest pride. He still pined for Skye but he was piping again, and for an audience who knew what good piping was.

Jamie's regular duties included scrubbing the floors and furniture of the sick bay with warm vinegar twice a week, giving medicine to the sick, and sounding a daily call on deck for sores to be dressed. When he finished, he would go to the surgeon's cabin to do odd jobs and learn treatments— so far mostly for ship fever, exhaustion and frostbite. Surgeon Wackley was especially proud of a great jagged saw with several broken teeth.

"You use that on the patients?" Jamie quavered when he first saw it.

"Only when they're fractious," beamed the surgeon. "It quietens them down wonderfully."

To his surprise, Jamie had no trouble with these lessons and Surgeon Wackley often complimented him on his quickness. He wished his father could be there to hear it. The surgeon was a kind man but a poor sailor. The ship, endlessly creaking and groaning, tossed in even mild seas and the North Atlantic was seldom mild. Like Angus and many others on board, he suffered from violent bouts of seasickness.

"Next to a toothache this is the worst ill that can beset a man," he moaned one particularly wild day when even his favourite cure of a pint of strong white ale—piping hot with a handful of tansy boiled in it—had failed him.

He glared feebly at Jamie. "Why are you never stricken? Have you sold your soul to the Devil?" He brightened. "D'you suppose he'd take mine?"

Jamie set down the boots which he had polished to a

high gloss. Despite his disreputable jacket, the surgeon was very particular about his boots.

"My father always said I had a cast-iron stomach. And it's time for you to get up and dress for dinner."

Wackley struggled reluctantly from his hammock and reached for his crumpled jacket. "I suppose you're right. What's this I hear about you being the son of a dangerous Jacobite? If you're going to murder me in my bed, then I'd be grateful if you'd do it when I'm having one of these damnable attacks of seasickness."

As he wrestled with his boots, Wackley went on. "You speak Gaelic with the Highlanders, French with their officers, English with the rest of us, and I've seen you reading one of my books in Latin. Which is your first language? What I would call your mother tongue?"

"My father used to wonder about that, too. He told me when I was a child and got hurt, I would cry in Gaelic. So he decided that must be my mother tongue."

"I'd like to meet your father someday—in peaceful circumstances," said Wackley. He stood up cautiously, turned pale and sat down again. "What else did he teach you?"

"To play backgammon."

"What an enlightened man." The surgeon looked wistfully around the cabin. "What a pity we don't have a set. I have a great weakness for games of chance. Confidentially, that's the reason I'm here. I gambled too much in my youth, and my father sent me to sea."

"I have a travelling set that my father made for me."

"I knew he was enlightened," beamed Wackley. "We

must play. Set up the board, but promise me that no matter how I plead or threaten, you will refuse to let me bet. It's a disease. Always ready to break out again and destroy me." Two patches of red mottled his ashen cheeks, and his eyes were feverishly bright. "Are you a good player?"

"I won my last game, but I haven't played for four months." Jamie thought about the night of his birthday, and the faces of his friends in Normandy began to float through his memory.

"Don't daydream, boy," said the surgeon impatiently, setting out the pieces. "We just have enough time for a game before dinner."

"My move, I think."

They played during every spare moment for the next week.

"I'm almost afraid to say it, Jamie," the surgeon said one afternoon, "but ever since you produced that backgammon board I haven't been seasick. I think I'll write a paper for the Royal Society."

Later that same day, when Jamie came on deck on his way back from the sick bay, he found Angus staring over the starboard side.

"You can't see Skye from here."

"True enough, but were you ever seeing the likes of that?" Angus pointed to an island of ice in the distance. "They say that these can sink a ship, and it looks such a wee bit of a thing. We must be getting close to land. Did I tell you the news?" His fair skin had been flayed by wind and salt spray and his nose was peeling, but he grinned from ear to sunburnt ear.

"The Captain will be having me transferred to one of the Highland regiments as soon as we reach Halifax. He knows what a good piper is worth in battle. I'll be sorry to be leaving you and Willie, but I'm just not one for the King's navy. Willie is hoping that your uncle can send you both discharges before the French have a chance to blow your heads off."

"I was hoping that there'd be a chance to escape when we get to Halifax," said Jamie, pleased for Angus, but downcast at losing yet another friend. "But even if I did, I wouldn't know how to reach Virginia. I don't want to fight the French." He stared bleakly at the iceberg. "I don't want to fight anyone. I just want to find my father again."

"I have no cause to fight them either," said Angus, "but I have spent much of my life fighting without knowing why. Anyway, if you are ever needing a friend, remember me." He gave Jamie a friendly thump on the back that almost sent him overboard. "Someday we'll meet again. In happier times, you and Willie will be visiting me in Skye where the wind blows over seven glens and seven bens and seven mountain moors."

A few days later, land was sighted and a cheer rang through the ship. The stormy waters had taken their toll, three dead of ship fever and many too sick to walk. But fog and the great ice fields prevented them from landing, and the fleet had to follow the coast until reaching safe harbour in Halifax. The basin was already busy with small boats plying between the ships that had wintered there.

Soon after the *Stirling Castle* dropped anchor, Angus was rowed ashore to join his new regiment.

"We'll just have to wait and see what happens here," cautioned Willie as they leaned on the railing watching him. "At least we'll be on land for a bit and that will be a welcome change."

"I'll find out which merchant captains are in port," he continued. Wilson shambled by and he lowered his voice. "I may meet an old friend who can take us down the coast to Virginia, if help doesn't reach us from Archie."

"Jamie!" The shrill cry startled the hovering gulls.

"I'll meet you on shore later," said Willie. "The surgeon needs your help to get himself into the boat."

"Land at last," said Wackley as they stepped onto the dock. "Terra firma. I could happily spend the rest of my life here on the promise that I'd never have to go to sea again."

Jamie looked at the collection of weather-beaten wooden houses that straggled along the water's edge and shook his head, but he too enjoyed the feeling of solid ground under his feet. They walked unsteadily through the wide unpaved streets until the surgeon spotted a large building, three storeys high, surrounded by verandahs. "That's enough exercise for the moment," he said. "I'm stopping here at The Great Pontac for a bite to eat. You run off and see the rest of the town. You can come for me in two hours." He handed Jamie a coin, "Get yourself something too."

Jamie thanked him and wandered off among the soldiers, sailors, and townspeople who made the town bustle with activity. He came to a street where every other shop contained either a grogseller or a fight, bought a pork pie and ate it while he walked. There were uniforms he'd never seen, and Indians and gaunt leather-clad men with small axes stuck in their belts stalking by. He noticed a man sitting in a pit while others shovelled dirt on top of him until only his head stuck out of the ground. He seemed very cheerful.

"What's he being punished for?"

The grenadier beside Jamie laughed. "He isn't being punished. It's a cure for scurvy. He'll stay there for a few hours each day until he's cured. They say it never fails."

After a while Jamie decided that his two hours must be just about up and started back to The Great Pontac. He found Surgeon Wackley on the verandah, talking to a resplendent officer. When Jamie got closer he decided that he must be an admiral, judging by the lace and gold braid that foamed and glittered on his blue-velvet coat and three-cornered hat. As Jamie waited—at a safe distance— he noticed three young midshipmen standing to one side. They must be attending the admiral. Two were older: one was tall and spindly as a grasshopper, the other, short and stout. The third, a fair-haired stocky boy, was about his own age. The older midshipmen were teasing him. Poking and elbowing, but making sure that the admiral couldn't see what was happening.

Jamie drifted closer and heard the spindly one say, "Your trouble, Douglas, is that you don't stand up for yourself."

The older boys had their backs to Jamie. The young

midshipman was facing them. Jamie picked up a small cask beside the tavern door and quietly set it down behind the two. Then he crept away.

The young midshipman smiled when he saw the opportunity. He waited until Jamie was clear, then lunged at his tormentors. They had been expecting this and stepped back, laughing. Their expressions changed from glee to shock as they fell together over the cask, flat on their backs in the mud.

"What are you two doing?" The admiral glared down at them. "Get back to the ship before I have you taken there in irons."

They fled.

The admiral returned to his conversation with Surgeon Wackley. "It's agreed then. You can bring your loblolly boy with you. I take it that's the one," he said, nodding toward Jamie. "A resourceful young man you say. I notice that he handles casks with some skill." There was the trace of a smile on his face as he bid the surgeon good day. "We sail within the week."

"Well, Jamie," said the surgeon as they trudged back to the ship. "I am sad to say we have been paid an honour. One of the surgeons on the *Princess Amelia* has the measles and I am to take his place immediately. It's sad because Admiral Durell's squadron is being sent ahead of the fleet as a vanguard. We will be sailing up the river toward Quebec, and I don't like arriving at battles any earlier than I have to. Pack your gear quickly, then come and help me to pack mine. Don't forget your backgammon board," he added.

As soon as he had clambered aboard the *Stirling Castle*, Jamie ran to find Willie. "What do we do now?" he asked after he had explained. "There won't be any chance to escape with an admiral waiting for me."

"We don't have much choice," said Willie, who seemed unsure of himself for once. "You'll have to go. I'll get word to you somehow when I find a way out. Just stay close to Wackley and the sick bay. Don't go trying to be a hero and getting killed. Your Uncle Archie wouldn't like that."

"Give me a hand, my boy. I always have trouble getting aboard," said Wackley as they reached the *Princess Amelia*. "I might even like the navy if it weren't for the sea and the ships."

But once they were on board, the surgeon approved of his new quarters. "A bit more room here than in the *Stirling Castle*. Now we should inspect the sick bay."

The sick bay, up in the bow of the main deck, was clean and empty. "Just the way I like to see it. Why don't you bunk here? It will be crowded below and until we need these quarters for the sick you might as well enjoy the space. Come to my cabin in half an hour and help me to unpack my books."

After Surgeon Wackley left, Jamie surveyed his new domain. He unrolled his pack, shook out his Normandy clothes and felt in the seams of his coat to make sure that the coins he had left were still there. Then he reached into the secret pocket he had made for his father's snuffbox.

He was looking at the miniature painting of his mother when he heard a sound. Jamie slid the snuffbox back into its hiding place. The young midshipman he had helped at the tavern stuck his head round the door.

"Can I come in?"

"Only if you're not sick," said Jamie. "We aren't taking any customers 'til tomorrow."

The boy came forward. "I'm George Douglas. I came to thank you. I've wanted to do something like that to Francis and Viat for months. They're not bad really, but they tease me a lot. This is my first voyage and I get homesick, but I don't get seasick," he added with a grin.

"I'm Jamie Macpherson."

"I have to go on watch now," said George. "I'd like to talk to you again about the work you do. I'm trying to learn what everyone does on the ship."

When George left, Jamie carefully repacked his belongings and went to find Surgeon Wackley's cabin.

After he had arranged the books and supplies to the surgeon's satisfaction, they settled down to enjoy a game of backgammon.

"I had a visit from the midshipman who was with the admiral," Jamie said.

"The one being teased by the two middies?"

"I didn't think you saw that."

"Admiral Durell noticed what you were up to. He had a difficult time keeping a straight face when he heard the crash. Young George Douglas is his nephew. He tries not to favour the boy. It isn't easy to be a midshipman on your uncle's ship."

82

"He didn't say that the admiral was his uncle."

"He probably wants to be known as George Douglas and not as the admiral's nephew," said the surgeon, "and that is a point in his favour. A four and a two, and I just won a game for a change." A crafty look crept across his face. "What say we make a small wager on the next game? My ruffled shirt for your dirk?"

"No," Jamie said firmly.

The trip to the St. Lawrence took far longer than Jamie had expected. First they made their way back along the coast of Nova Scotia until they cleared Cape Breton. Then they seemed to be back on the ocean again. Jamie kept asking when they would reach the river until someone told him they were already on it. After four days of fair winds he finally had a sense of being on a river, but it still amazed him with its width. Now he could see the rugged country on the north shore. Jamie leaned on the starboard rail watching a shoal of porpoises swimming alongside the ship.

"The French will know we're on the way now," said George, joining him at the rail. Despite many pointed remarks from Viat and Francis about a midshipman wasting his time with a loblolly boy, he and Jamie had become good friends.

"Are we likely to have a battle?"

"Why do you ask? Is it because you want a chance to be a hero and hope the French will attack, or because you are afraid and hope that they won't? No offence," George added quickly. "I ask too many questions. It's a habit that gets me in trouble."

"I get in trouble by giving too many answers," said Jamie.

"I haven't heard you giving any answers," George replied. "You're as talkative as a clam. What do you think about when you stare at the water? Are you homesick?"

Jamie laughed, but stopped quickly when George looked hurt.

"I'm not laughing at anyone else feeling homesick," he said. "It's just that I've moved so often I don't think I have a home. I miss my father and I often think about a village in Normandy and my friends there. When I get really lonely I think of my mother. I don't remember her, but I can imagine her through my father's memories and a picture of her that he gave me. The English killed her."

A long pause. George gazed at the frolicking porpoises, searching for help. "What will you do if there's a battle?"

"I'll do my best to help the wounded."

George smiled with relief. "I was worried that I was going to have to ask, 'friend or foe?'"

7
Foe
May 1759

Up near the bow with Old Tom Growling, Jamie leaned on the rail, watching a row of cormorants standing on a rock, shaking their wings in the wind to dry them. Tom was the midshipmen's "boy", which meant he kept their untidy quarters shipshape as best he could. He had been at sea since he was nine years old, but no one knew how long ago that was. His age was the one thing that Tom swore he couldn't remember. He had sailed everywhere and was the only man aboard who had been up the St. Lawrence before.

One sailor was calling out soundings. A midshipman was perched in the cross-trees taking bearings. "It gets more dangerous upstream," Tom said to Jamie. "The channel, it do keep a-shiftin', and if you don't know the river you can be 'igh and dry on a sandbar afore you know it. The Old Man, he'll need all 'is wits about 'im." He gave a toothless grin and spat into the water.

Off the port bow, a headland jutted out from the south shore. As they came closer Jamie made out a settlement in the shelter of a great rock that rose like the prow of a ship. The sailor was called in from the bowsprit, and the order was given for silence on deck. Tom nudged Jamie and pointed to the mast, where Jamie was startled to see the French colours flying. "He be a crafty devil, the Old Man."

They watched the shore and soon saw canoes heading out to the *Princess Amelia*. When they arrived alongside, the Canadian pilots were welcomed aboard. In French. Once he had the pilots he needed for the next stage of the river, the admiral struck the French colours and hoisted the British flag. This brought cheers from the crew and curses from the Canadian river pilots.

Bic slowly faded into the distance behind them and Jamie went below, back to work. "Well, Jamie, what is happening on the river?" asked Surgeon Wackley. "Any sign of the French?"

"Yes, sir. They boarded the ship at Bic."

"What?" He looked up from cutting his toenail with a scalpel. "Never make clever remarks to a man with a knife," he said, waving the scalpel at Jamie.

"Sorry, sir, it wasn't meant to be smart. The admiral tricked the Canadian river pilots into coming aboard at Bic, and now they will have to guide us up the river. You see, the river shifts its sandbars—"

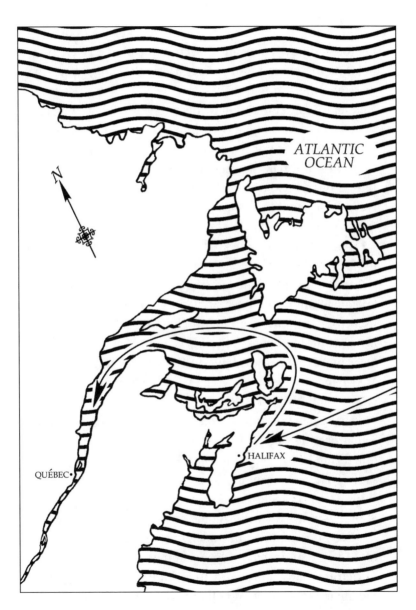

ATLANTIC
OCEAN

QUÉBEC•

• HALIFAX

HALIFAX TO QUEBEC

"Enough, enough. First you almost make me cut off my big toe and now you want to lecture me on the river. Just help me to get ready for dinner, then you can go back to watching the fish."

Jamie had been about to describe the beluga whales which Old Tom had shown him earlier in the day, but decided this was not the time.

As darkness fell, they anchored for the night. A bonfire flared on the south shore and, back on deck, Jamie watched a signal light flashing an answer from the top of a headland on the north shore.

"They're keeping track of us now," said George, joining him at the rail.

It was an odd friendship this, between a loblolly boy and an admiral's nephew, but George was a friendly soul, used to going birdnesting and climbing with the stable-boys at the Hall back home in Devon. Viat and Francis were more inclined to stand on ceremony, but they tolerated Jamie—when they weren't teasing him as a Jacobite and a stubborn Scot.

Day by day the shores grew closer. And every night the signal fires flashed their warning. They could see burned out farmhouses. "Signs of war," Surgeon Wackley said sadly. When the vanguard reached Île aux Coudres, the ships dropped anchor.

"How much further?" Jamie asked the next morning.

"I've no idea, but I'm told we're within seventy miles of Quebec and that's close enough for me. Colonel Tarleton went ashore with light infantry yesterday, but the inhabitants had vanished across the Narrows and into the hills of the north shore. They left in such a hurry that there were fires burning in their hearths and loaves of bread baking in their ovens."

With land so near, the midshipmen grew restless and badgered Josiah Conder, the grim-faced gunner who was in charge of them, to let them explore the island. After he had given grudging permission, George came racing down to the sick bay.

"Come on, Lob, we're going ashore." He stopped and stared at Jamie, who sat on a bed, wearing his ordinary clothes. "What are you up to? You're not planning to jump ship, are you?"

"Nothing so brave," said Jamie. "Just washing my navy gear." At the other side of the sick bay his shirt, trousers, and stockings were hanging on a line.

"Well come as you are," said George. "You look like a Canadian in that outfit. We can pretend that we captured you."

Jamie got permission to go with the midshipmen. "Take a blanket," said the surgeon. "The fog's thick as buttermilk around the river, and it's still early enough in the year for a cold night. I don't expect you to get lost, but it wouldn't surprise me if one of the midshipmen did."

Jamie rolled his shoes up in his coat and plaid, tied the pack and slung it over his shoulder. He thought of the trunks he packed and unpacked for Surgeon Wackley when they changed ships. "It certainly makes life easier when everything you own can be rolled into a plaid," Jamie thought.

When he climbed down to the dinghy, George said, "Now you really do look like a runaway."

"Doctor's orders," replied Jamie.

Tom rowed them into the shallow water. While Jamie waded ashore, slithering on the seaweed-covered rocks, Tom carried the others on his back, like an ancient turtle, one by one over the freezing water to the beach.

Île aux Coudres was shrouded in silence. The only sounds came from the bees gathering nectar and the circling seagulls arguing endlessly with the wind.

"Come back for us at sundown," Viat told the seaman. "We need time to explore."

"Shouldn't we be back sooner?" George asked, scrambling to dry land.

"Scared of being left in the dark?" asked Francis as he lumbered through tidal pools and clumps of seagrass that bristled like green pincushions. His passage disturbed a long-legged heron who flapped away in fright.

"I'm not scared," said George indignantly.

"Leave him alone," said Viat. "Let's explore."

The boys wandered aimlessly along the track that ran beside the river. Often there were the remains of signal fires. They passed a small white church and several squat, stone, wayside crosses. George and Viat were jumping back and forth across the ditch which ran beside the track, and Jamie was skipping flat stones over the water, when Francis saw the stone house crouched on the bluff above them.

"Take cover," he shouted, and leapt into the ditch.

Everyone jumped in beside him. "What is it? The

90

French? What did you see?"

"There's a house on the hill up there. It may be occupied."

"Let's move on," suggested George.

"Come on, George," said Viat. "Can't you tell when he isn't serious? I vote that we attack, and capture the enemy fort for England."

"All right, my lads," said Francis. "A frontal assault, but we must surprise them. The first man to make a sound gets a flogging after the battle."

Jamie watched them crawl awkwardly through the bushes and start up the slope toward the house. "They're like ducks," he thought, "fine on water but not very impressive on land." He smiled, remembering the cliffs of Normandy where he and Gilles had clambered like goats. "This is my territory." He stowed his pack under a bush and ran along the track to a spot where the slope, studded with a small orchard of apple trees, was easier to climb. He scrambled up quickly, keeping out of sight of the others.

The three intrepid attackers kept slipping back down the sandy slope, but by clutching at clumps of grass and the roots of bushes they finally reached the top and lay panting on the grass near the front of the house. Francis motioned to Viat and George.

"Attack!" and they charged through the door.

The room echoed with the clatter of their boots on the bare floor. Secretly, they were relieved to find the house empty but were careful not to show it. They stared around the silent room: at the massive stone fireplace and the small wooden cradle in the corner beside a carved chest. Then Francis stood on a chair and announced, "I claim this house in the name of the King."

"La France!" Jamie dropped through the trap door from the loft above.

Francis fell off the chair, scrambled to his feet and bolted out the door, closely followed by Viat, with George a step behind. Francis and Viat couldn't stop in time and rolled over the edge, slithering and sliding all the way to the bottom of the hill. George managed to stop and glanced back to see the enemy before jumping. When he saw Jamie he roared with indignation.

"You miserable Jacobite! How did you get up there?" Then he looked at the bedraggled pair at the bottom of the slope and started to laugh.

"Jump, George, jump!" they shouted. Jamie came out of the house and sat on the edge of the bluff with him. He waved to the two below. "A well executed retreat," he called.

The wind caught the open door behind them and slammed it shut with the noise of a cannon. George and Jamie fell over the edge and tumbled all the way down, landing at the others' feet. This pleased Francis and Viat so much that they forgot how angry they were.

After Jamie had retrieved his pack, they dusted themselves off and continued along the hard sand of the shore, exploring the island. As they strolled along, each in turn explained that he hadn't been scared, but the midshipmen agreed that Jamie had won the battle.

Then George saw a windmill and they headed inland

toward it. They walked for a long time and discovered that it was further away than it looked from the shore. A mist was beginning to creep over the island. Jamie remembered from Normandy how quickly a sea fog could make the world disappear. "Maybe we should turn back. We can go tomorrow."

"Now who's scared?" said Francis. "We'll get there if we race. Jamie has his pack and George is the smallest, so Viat and I will give you a head start. We'll count to two hundred and then be after you. Go."

George and Jamie ran as fast as they could, up the grassy hills and through the trees.

"They'll catch us for certain," George panted. Jamie cast a hurried look over his shoulder but couldn't see Viat or Francis.

"Where have they got to?" said George as he slumped down on the grass.

"Perhaps it's an enchanted island," Jamie said, joining him. "And everyone will vanish. Remember those stories the pilot from Bic told us, about all the sorcerers and witches in Quebec?"

"Let's keep on for the windmill then. It isn't far. I can hear it creaking."

"The mist is getting thicker. I think we should go back."

"Ay-ee-ee-ee!" Shrieking like banshees, Viat and Francis swept past, riding bareback on two horses.

They tugged at the horses' manes to bring them to a halt and waited for Jamie and George to catch up.

"Where did you find them?" George asked, stroking

the shaggy neck of one of the horses. It was a small sturdy creature, brown and black-maned, with large wild eyes. "I haven't ridden for nearly a year. Give me a turn, please."

"Swing yourself up behind me," said Francis. "Lob, you give him a leg up."

As they trotted off, Viat called back to Jamie, "We'll meet you at the shore."

They headed toward a thick band of fog that veiled the trees. The river had vanished entirely.

Crack! Crack! Crack!

The shots came just as the horses reached the fog bank. They reared up on their hind legs and the riders were thrown off, invisible in the fog. Jamie started running.

As he came closer, he heard voices. Then he saw that the midshipmen were on their feet. Surrounded by men in homespun. With muskets! He slowed down but was going too fast to stop before one of the men turned around.

"*Avancez!*" He pointed his musket and Jamie obeyed. They had been captured by a band of Canadian militia.

"You don't look like this crew," the Canadian continued in French, staring from the midshipmen's cocked hats and ruffled shirts to Jamie's battered breeches. "What are you doing here?"

Jamie thought rapidly. It would do no good for him to be a prisoner too. A moment's hesitation and, "I'm from Bic," he replied, in French.

"And how does a boy from Bic come to be with English sailors on Île aux Coudres?"

Jamie remembered the angry faces of the trapped Canadians at Bic. "My uncle is...a river pilot, and he was

94

tricked into going out to the English ship. I was with him.... They made us stay on board and guide the ship up the river. These boys wanted to have some fun on the island today, and they ordered me to come along. I thought I might have a chance to slip away and make my way home." As he spoke Jamie prayed that none of the men came from Bic.

"If you wanted to escape, why didn't you run the other way when you saw them fall?" the Canadian persisted.

Jamie shrugged. "You hear a shot, and you try to help someone. I don't know why I ran this way and not the other. Maybe I'm as stupid as my uncle. He went out to help an English ship just because it flew a French flag."

The others had turned to listen, and one who seemed to be in command said, "He may be telling the truth." He studied Jamie's face as if memorizing it. "Do any of them speak French?"

George, Francis, and Viat had been trying to follow what was being said, but they could only understand one word in ten in the rapidly spoken exchange. Viat decided that Jamie was in league with the enemy, and that he had somehow arranged their capture. He adopted his haughtiest air. "In the navy we shoot French spies," he told him. "It will give me great pleasure to see that you get what you deserve."

This was delivered with such conviction that the Canadians accepted Jamie's story. Their leader turned to Viat with mock seriousness and in careful English said, "Then by your rules, I feel obliged to order my men to shoot you."

Viat went white but stood his ground. "We are prisoners. You can't shoot us."

One of the other men spoke. "Captain des Rivières, we have no time for all this talk. These children are worthless as prisoners."

Viat understood only part of this conversation and decided they were to be shot after all. He pointed to George. "He is the nephew of Admiral Durell, Second-in-Command of His Majesty's fleet. We are officers and gentlemen and demand to be treated as such."

The men looked more amused than impressed when this was translated by their leader. "We'll take them to Quebec," he decided. "And you," he smiled pleasantly but Jamie wondered if he was convinced, "will come with us. It would be too dangerous to try to return to Bic from here. We were sent to get details about the movements of the English fleet. The prisoners will supply the information we need, and you may be able to confirm what they tell us."

One of the men spoke up. "We should be off before the English start looking for their little officers."

They tied George, Francis, and Viat together in the same way that Jamie had been roped to Willie and Angus by the press gang. He smiled ruefully at the memory.

"There's no need to mock us," George said coldly.

Jamie followed along after the group. The Canadians moved as silently as cats, and he realized that he would have about as much chance as the midshipmen to escape in these dark woods where giant tree roots snaked through the mud, grappling the rocks like iron bands. He would have to tag along and explain to George later that he hadn't turned from friend to foe in an afternoon.

They were marched over an all but invisible path until at last they emerged from the woods and scrambled down to a small cove where a large canoe was hidden in the underbrush. The Canadians carried it to the water, and the prisoners were placed in the centre. Jamie saw that the midshipmen were starting to shiver. The rapid walk through the woods had helped to work out the stiffness from their fall from the horses, but now the cold night air on the river was chilling them to the marrow. He untied his pack, unrolled his plaid, and wrapped it around the three shivering boys, ignoring their scowls.

"They can't help you if they're frozen," he said to the captain. He put on his own coat, hung his shoes round his neck, and got into the canoe.

"What's your name?" asked the captain.

"Jacques—Jacques Leblanc." The canoe moved silently into the stream.

8

The Fortune Teller

June 1759

They stopped three times during the night. Always in a sheltered bay. While the men smoked their pipes, the yawning boys walked around to get the stiffness out of their legs. Then back into the canoe, and the steady paddling rhythm began again.

Jamie fell into a restless sleep and wakened with the warm sun on his head. Viat lay with his long legs twisted under him and a scowl on his face. Francis was snoring and George was curled up in a ball. At first Jamie was dazzled by the sun on the water, then slowly, through the shimmer and the mist, he saw Quebec. The great rock dominating the river. The buildings of Upper Town crowded to the edge of the cliff like spectators. Below were the houses of Lower Town, huddled between the base of the cliff and the river.

The midshipmen were awake now too, silently staring at the batteries of guns and the fortified city. They tried not to look impressed, but their eyes betrayed them.

"Have you been here before?" asked the captain.

"No," said Jamie, glad to be answering truthfully for a change. "I've never seen anything like it."

"A natural fortress, as I'm sure our young officers would agree if they could understand French."

"We'll still take it," said George, who had been watching Quebec grow nearer. "But it will be a tough nut to crack," he muttered to himself.

"Bravely spoken." Captain des Rivières turned back to Jamie. "We'll take the prisoners to the fort, but I want you to go to Champlain Street in Lower Town, to a fortune teller called Heli. He's an old friend of mine. Everyone knows him in the Quarter. I will meet you there later. Give him a message from me. He is to tell your fortune."

When Jamie looked surprised, he added, "It's a joke between us. He'll understand. Just tell him that Captain des Rivières sent you."

As they came closer to the dock the rock loomed higher above the thicket of stone houses and warehouses below. When they landed Jamie rolled up his pack and watched the midshipmen being marched off to Upper Town. There was no chance to explain. Francis and Viat brushed by without speaking, Viat looking straight ahead and Francis glowering. George hesitated, as if to speak, then bolted past. Jamie stared after them. "I'll get a message to them later. Somehow. But first I'd better find this fortune teller," he said to no one.

He asked directions from a passing sailor and was soon threading his way along a narrow street, through crowds of people. Feeble old men and scrawny urchins were hard at work preparing defences against the enemy that was sailing toward them. Sounds of hammering and sawing echoed in the air.

"Upper Town may be safe," Jamie thought, "but I wouldn't want to be down here when the British cannon starts its barrage."

"I'm looking for Heli, the fortune teller," he said to a husky young woman who was energetically brushing the cobbles in front of her house.

"That one." She pointed across the street to a narrow house with a dormer in its slanting roof. A small red cat slept on the window ledge.

He knocked on the door. No one answered.

"You have to go in," she called.

He knocked again, waited, then opened the door. The room was dark after the sunlight outside. An old man sat by the low fire that glimmered in the hearth.

"Captain des—" Jamie was shushed into silence by a girl, about his own age, who sat half-hidden on the other side of the old man's rocking chair.

The old man continued talking. He was telling a ghost story. It was filled with witches, devils and werewolves, and despite the sunny day outside, Jamie felt stabs of fear as the tale unfolded. When it ended, he and the girl both shivered at the same time. The old man chuckled and lit his long clay pipe.

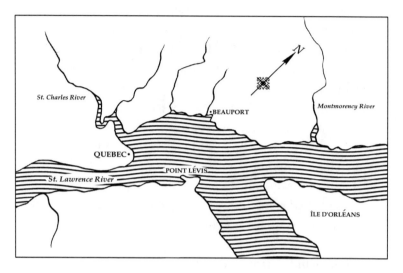

QUEBEC AND ENVIRONS

"I like a good audience."

Jamie had wondered if Heli the fortune teller would be a strange creature with glittering mad eyes and a houseful of black cats. He was relieved to find a cheerful man, with a mass of snowy curls and a face seamed as an oak tree, who enjoyed telling stories.

"Captain des Rivières sent me with a message. He'll be here later and—" Jamie hesitated.

"Go on," said Heli, now wreathed in smoke rings.

"He said that he wanted you to tell my fortune. He said you'd understand."

Heli smiled. "I can tell that you are not sure that you understand. Don't worry. Come over to the light and let me see what you look like. I'm Heli and this is Jeanne, my granddaughter."

"And that's Minette," added the girl. The small ginger cat leapt down from the window onto Jeanne's lap and began to purr loudly while it cleaned a cream-striped paw. Jamie noticed that it had six toes.

"I'm Jacques...Leblanc from Bic."

"All the way from Bic," said Heli reflectively. "Let's see your bundle there."

Jamie was reluctant to part with it. "If I'm to tell your fortune I need something of yours to hold, something that has a strong sense of you about it. Don't worry, I won't keep it."

Jamie handed over the pack.

Heli unrolled the blanket and felt the cloth. "Fine wool," he said. Then he unfolded Jamie's coat, and put the shoes on the floor beside the blanket. "Have you anything here that I could use to get a sense of you?"

"No, I don't think so." Jamie didn't want the old man to search through the coat and find the secret pocket with his father's snuffbox. "What about this?" He drew the dirk from his belt.

Heli took the knife. "A fine piece of steel. The gift of a fond father or stolen from a gentleman of taste."

"It is my father's and was my grandfather's before him," Jamie said indignantly.

"Well, Jacques," said Heli, "before I try to see into your future I should tell you something of your past."

He held the dirk in his hands and closed his eyes, considering. The only sounds in the room were the creaking of the rocker and the purring of the cat. "I cannot see Bic at all. I see a village in France. I see a Jacobite father but no mother. Then there is a great journey full of danger and adventure. Now I see a red flag. You are in the British navy. It starts to dim. I see you captured by a band of *habitants* and brought to Quebec by canoe."

He opened his eyes and sat up. Jeanne let out a low hiss and started toward Jamie. "An English spy!"

Jamie headed toward the door but Jeanne moved quickly to block his escape.

"Easy now," said Heli. "I'm only an old fortune teller, not a judge. Jeanne, be quiet and sit down. I want to talk to our guest, not frighten him to death." She dragged over a chair and sat down, hard, in front of the door.

"We can start with your name."

"Jamie Macpherson. How could you see the past so clearly?"

"That's my secret, but I'll tell you anyway," said the fortune teller. "Your plaid, your shoes, the coins sewn in your coat, and the designs on your knife, none of these is a sign of a boy from Bic. Yet your French is as good as mine, so where did you come from and how did you get here? If my friend, the captain, sent you, then he picked you up on one of his trips downriver. The rest is deduction."

"My father alive and my mother dead. How did you know that?"

"Simple. You said the dirk *is* your father's, not *was*, so he is still alive. And I did not say that your mother was dead, only that I couldn't *see* her. You supplied the rest.

Now that I've told you all my secrets why don't you tell me a few of yours."

"First, I'm not a spy," said Jamie emphatically. "I travelled from France to Scotland to find my uncle, but I was press-ganged into the British navy before I found him. I didn't want to be a sailor, and I didn't want to fight the French, but I was put on the admiral's ship when it sailed up the river from Halifax. When we reached Île aux Coudres, I went ashore with three midshipmen who were captured. I thought that I might be allowed to go free if I said I was a boy from Bic. Then I thought I could go back to the ship for help. I've done a lot of stupid things, but I'm not an English spy. I'm not a French spy either," he added ruefully, remembering the angry faces of the midshipmen.

"You are in the British navy and in enemy country in disguise. That makes you a spy. You even tried to convince us that you were Canadian," said Heli. "If it walks like a duck, quacks like a duck, and flies like a duck, then it's a duck. So you are a spy."

Jamie sat down on a stool and held his head in his hands.

There was a knock on the door. Jeanne moved her chair and the Captain came in.

"All right," said Jamie defiantly. "You can shoot me, but I'm not a spy."

The Captain laughed when Heli told him what had happened.

"I knew there was something strange about the boy, and I wanted to find out what he was up to. You don't meet many sons of pilots who have never been in a canoe. And why should the British midshipmen be surprised and angry when a boy from Bic is friendly with his Canadian rescuers?

"You have managed to be condemned by both sides in the space of twenty-four hours," he continued. "You have a rare talent for self-destruction."

"Let's have some food while we think about this tangle," said Heli. "Jeanne, could you find something for us? You'd better help her," he said to Jamie. "That way you can make sure that she doesn't poison you."

"English spy," she said with venom. "I could understand you being a soldier, but a spy is worse than a—a toad."

"I'm not English," he reminded her. "I'm Scots."

"English. Scottish. Shot from one kills us just as dead as shot from the other." She began to pull plates and cutlery from a large wooden chest.

Heli and the captain sat smoking companionably by the fire. "What's to be done with him?" the fortune teller asked. "He's the most unlikely spy I've ever seen."

The captain blew a smoke ring and watched Minette chase it across the room. "If I take him to the fort, they'll have him shot as an example to others," he said slowly. "Why don't you keep him here—if he'll give his word not to escape. You say his father is a Highlander. Pledge him on his father's honour."

When Jeanne and Jamie brought the meal—bread and watery soup—Heli told Jamie what had been decided, and he accepted their offer gratefully.

"We'll put you in Jeanne's keeping," Heli said.

"I'd rather face the firing squad," Jamie replied, and then dodged the wooden spoon that crashed down where his head had been.

"I declare a truce," said Heli. "I don't like bloodshed when I'm eating."

After their meal, Jamie asked about the midshipmen. "I feel badly that I'll be free to walk about the town while they're locked up in a dungeon, shivering and starving."

Captain des Rivières laughed. "Don't feel sorry for them. They'll be treated as the toast of the town, given parole on their word as officers, and fed much better than you."

"The Upper Town still eats well," said Heli, "but if the British can read the river, the Governor's menu will soon be the same as ours."

"Horsemeat and gruel," Jeanne said darkly.

"What do you mean, read the river?" asked Jamie.

"Some say the British will never reach Quebec, that the river is too difficult to navigate without a skilled pilot."

"But they have the pilots from Bic."

"The pilots would guide the British away from Bic, like small birds leading a hawk away from their nests. But they would never show the enemy the channel to take them past Île d'Orléans, the Traverse," said Heli. "They will have to find it themselves, and that could take weeks or even months."

"What if they do find the channel?" asked Jamie.

"The guns of Quebec will blow them out of the water. They could capture Île d'Orléans, but we will sit on the high ground and laugh at them until the winter threatens to freeze the river and they have to sail away empty-handed," said the captain.

Heli smiled sadly. "But if they capture Île d'Orléans, they will do much damage before the winter comes to save us. And the winter won't be our friend for long. The British will destroy the harvest before they go, and to-night's meagre supper will seem like a feast when we remember it."

"Fortune tellers love a gloomy story," said the captain, rising to his feet. "I must return to the fort. Don't let him frighten you with tales of death and destruction."

During the next few days Jeanne kept a close and hostile eye on Jamie as he helped her with her chores. Once she decided that he was going to keep his word not to escape, she allowed him to wander around Lower Town. It was a busy place where everyone seemed to know everyone else. The people were friendly, but Jamie noticed a growing fear of the approaching British ships. News and rumours spread quickly as a plague from the docks through the rat's tangle of back alleys. A British cutter had been captured off Île d'Orléans. The British pilots had charted the mysterious Traverse in less time than anyone thought possible and the main force could not be far behind.

Twice each week Jeanne went to Upper Town to deliver goods to the Ursuline Convent. "I saw your friends again today," she said to Jamie at supper. "Two strutting fools who act as if they had conquered Quebec all by themselves, and a quiet fair-haired one who sits alone on the ramparts waiting for his fleet to arrive."

Jamie looked at Heli. "Can I go with Jeanne next time? The quiet one was my friend. I'd like a chance to explain to him that I'm not a French spy."

"You can go, but don't let the others see you. Don't tell him where you live either, or you may find a dragoon waiting for you in Champlain Street. Then we'd all be in trouble."

The next afternoon Jeanne and Jamie climbed past the sentries on Palace Hill to Upper Town. All the other roads from Lower Town had been blocked. When they reached the top, they rested on the ramparts and watched the river spread out below them. Small boats cut like water beetles through the flashes of sunlight on the water. It was hard to believe that a battle fleet was gathering on the other side of the island just down the river. As they walked along the ramparts, the Saint Charles River came into view, and they could see supplies moving across the bridge to the French troops on the Beauport shore.

"General Wolfe will get a warm welcome if he tries to land over there," Jamie said.

"If he does, we'll come up here and watch your general get his head blown off."

"Bloodthirsty savage. And he's not my general."

"English spy."

"Enough. Where are we likely to see George?"

"He comes to the wall in the afternoon and watches the troops crossing to Beauport. There he is up ahead."

They came up behind George as he sat on the cannon-studded wall staring down at the bridge. Jamie scarcely recognized him. His short blue jacket had been replaced by a linen shirt and a scarlet sash of silk.

"I've brought my prisoner to talk to you."

George turned round, startled by this brisk outburst of French from a strange girl. He looked even more startled when he saw Jamie. "Excuse me," he said to Jeanne in his halting French. "Did you say prisoner?"

Jeanne looked sternly at Jamie. "Sit down, English spy."

Jamie was so surprised that he obeyed instantly. Only he sat on grass still wet from the morning rain and promptly jumped up again. Jeanne was delighted at his confusion. She laughed and Jamie grinned.

"I don't understand any of this," George complained, trying very hard not to grin himself.

Jamie explained what had happened on Île aux Coudres and how he too was a prisoner. "On my father's honour." He spoke French because he wanted Jeanne to understand everything he said. This caused some difficulties for George, and Jamie had to repeat a few words in English. He remembered Heli's warning and said nothing about Lower Town. "Don't tell Francis and Viat that we met. They wouldn't believe me, and I'm in enough trouble now without any they might cause. I wanted you to know, but I don't care what they believe."

George looked despondent when Jamie mentioned the others. "I never see them. You wouldn't believe it, Lob. Every day there are parties and banquets and gambling. Francis and Viat are off most afternoons and nights on picnics and pony-cart rides. They're running up gambling debts, too. They've told everyone that while I'm the nephew of an admiral, they're the sons of a great milord."

"Fools!" Jamie said bitterly, remembering Jeanne's worried face as she tried to scratch together a meal. He knew from grumbled conversations in the Quarter that Upper Town celebrated while Lower Town starved.

"Jamie." George seemed reluctant to say the words. "They've already sent a message to my uncle, denouncing you as a spy and a deserter. I'm glad to know that you aren't either. I'll write to him now but my message might not be delivered, and we're being sent to Trois Rivières tomorrow to join the other prisoners. When all this is over I'll tell my uncle too, but until I see him, you'd better stay away from the British navy."

"You talk as if the British will appear in Quebec any minute," said Jeanne crossly. "Don't you understand that Quebec can't be defeated by your ships and soldiers? Look at these cliffs, and over there at the Beauport shore." She pointed to the lines of white tents. "How can you defeat us?"

"I'm beginning to believe you're right," said George, "but you know the heights across the river, on the south shore?"

"Of course."

"The British will set up cannon on these heights and bombard the town." George spoke with such quiet certainty that Jeanne paled. "We may not win Quebec this time, but if we don't there won't be much left of the town when we leave."

"We have to go now." Jamie was anxious to get Jeanne

away before she attacked George. "I'm glad I had a chance to explain. Good luck."

George watched them leave, and then called after them, "Remember to stay away from the south shore when they start firing."

"Could they really fire all the way across the river?" asked Jeanne as they made their way back to Lower Town.

"I don't know, but if they do, we'll have a good view. I feel better now that George believes I'm not a French spy."

"And I no longer think you're an English spy." Jeanne could never stay depressed for long. "So when the British cannons drop bombs on your head you can die happy."

"Bloodthirsty savage," Jamie shouted after her as she ran into the house.

9
Fire Storms
July 1759

Jamie lifted the twitching fish from the basket and dumped them on the table. As quickly as he slapped them down, Madame Carrière sliced off their heads and tails and gutted them. When he started working for Heli's talkative neighbour, he had tried to pile the fish up faster than she could clean them. Now he knew better. She joked with her friends, argued with her customers, shifted the baskets to make Jamie's job easier, and all the while kept ahead of him in cleaning the fish. At the end of that first morning, she told him he was a good workman, but he should slow down a bit or he would drop dead before the day was out.

He had been working for three weeks. He started on the day after he talked to George on the ramparts. Every morning except Sunday, he got up at dawn and went to the river to move the baskets of fish from the few boats that still went out to Madame Carrière's stall at the market. When the whole British fleet arrived and anchored off Île d'Orléans in late June, the rich merchants of the town clogged the streets with wagonloads of their possessions, hurrying to the safety of the country. All the stall keepers left too, but "No Englishman," vowed Madame, "is going to stop *me* selling my fish. What would my ancestors say?"

Like every other male in Lower Town, Jamie would have worked for Madame Carrière for nothing. She was a beautiful whirlwind who blew life into the dullest of days or people. Her two passions were what went on in Lower Town and the exploits of her ancestors. Her black eyes blazed as she recounted how they had triumphed over bears, white rapids, Iroquois and werewolves. She could out-shout the carters when she was angry and she could make threats that turned sailors pale, but underneath, as Jamie quickly discovered, lurked the softest of hearts.

Every cat in the Quarter came round faithfully for the castoff heads and tails, and one of Jamie's tasks was to take a daily basket of fish to the sick and the poor.

Madame was convinced that the English were blackhearted demons. "They roast babies" she told Jamie. He didn't like to defend them in case she became suspicious. Heli had warned him not to betray himself to her or it would be all over the place, for "gossip flies around Quebec on wings."

When everything had been sold, he cleaned the stall and scrubbed the table ready for the next morning. Then he carried a basket of fish to Upper Town. Most of Madame's regular customers had left, but the sisters remained at the Ursuline Convent.

Jamie enjoyed going there because when they discovered that he could speak Latin, they insisted that all business be conducted in a half-serious, formal manner in that language. Afterwards they would give him a small treat from the kitchen. At first Jeanne was jealous of the special attention that the sisters paid to Jamie, but she cheered up when he shared his rewards with her. However, she wouldn't let him come into the house.

"You have to wash the fishy smell off first." And no matter how hard Jamie scrubbed himself she would hold her nose and bar the door.

He slapped the last two fish on the table and sat down.

"A good catch today," said Madame, fanning herself with her apron. "It's lucky the English can't scare the fish away. This morning I heard that Dumas is going to take old men and children across the river to chase the English from Lévis. I forbid you to go on such a stupid business. My ancestors would never have stood for it. It takes soldiers to fight soldiers, and I need you here. Anyway, an officer told me that we are not in any danger. When the English haul their cannons up to the heights of Lévis they'll soon discover that the river is too wide to fire across. Serve them right, the devils. May they fry in Hell."

Jamie looked across at the south shore as he had done many times since George's warning. It was close but still seemed a long way to fire a cannon. He hoped the French officer was right.

He had been asked to join Dumas' expedition to Lévis, and he was glad to have a good excuse not to go. What if he met Angus and his Highlanders in battle? That would really make him a traitor. The day before, he had watched the ragtag parade of volunteers march past—excited schoolboys, overweight shopkeepers, and old men—all on their way to "save Quebec." At the convent the sisters tried hard to be cheerful, but they were worried and even forgot to find him anything from the kitchen.

"The expedition tried to get across the river last night but couldn't," said Jamie. "I think they'll cross tonight."

"A good time to stay home," said Madame Carrière firmly.

That night he stared up at the stars from the hammock he had strung up behind the house. It was too hot to sleep. He tossed and turned and finally decided to take a walk down to the river where it would be cooler. He sat on a jetty, dangling his feet in the water. He could see the Lévis shore, a black silhouette against the sky. The bell from the Récollet chapel had just tolled the hour when out of the darkness he saw a flash. A noise like far-away thunder rumbled across the river. More flashes followed and the thunder rolls grew. Then he heard crashing sounds from the town behind him. "So George was right." After expecting the attack for so long he wondered how it could be a surprise. The thought brought him to his feet. Lower Town was being bombed by the cannons from the heights of Lévis.

Jamie ran back to warn Heli and Jeanne. The darkness hid the damage that had already been done to the town. As he turned the corner into Champlain Street, he fell over a pile of debris from the wall of a house hit by a cannon ball. There were voices in the darkness. A fire had started in the house next to Madame Carrière's. As the flames spread, the chaos in the street became visible in a ghostly orange light.

Jamie picked himself up, clambered over the remains of the wall, and ran desperately to Heli's house. By the light from the blazing buildings, he saw that it was unharmed, but he couldn't find Jeanne or Heli. He turned to see whether he could help anyone in the burning house.

The neighbours were gathering and had organized a bucket brigade. Jamie began to pass splashing, swinging buckets to the next person in the chain. They worked furiously until a voice called that the fire was out, but that someone was buried under the rubble. The human chain dropped the buckets, reversed its direction, and started passing stones hand to hand away from the bombed house until there was enough room for several people to dig into the rubble.

"Stop!" Heli stood with a torch alongside an opening that had been cleared in the pile of stones.

"The children are safe," he said, calming the crowd.

"They're at the back of the cellar. But Madame Carrière is pinned under a beam. We'll have to move the rest of the stones away very carefully, or the wall will collapse on top of her. Bring more torches. I need someone small to come forward, but not a child."

Jamie pushed his way through the crowd. "Will I do?"

"I'm doubly glad to see you, my boy. I thought the bombs had got you." Despite his cheerful manner, Heli's blue eyes were bleak. "Are you small enough to crawl through that hole? I need to know what is holding the beam up, and how we can raise it without bringing the rest down."

Jamie eased himself into the cavity, but the light from outside was not enough to show him how to proceed. He managed to turn and reached back toward Heli. "I need a light."

A torch was thrust into his hand and he pushed it ahead of him as he crawled deeper into the cave of stones. He could see how they supported one another, making a small arch over his head, and he prayed that he wouldn't bump the wrong one on his way past. The smoke from the torch burned his eyes as he tried to find the next twist in the tunnel.

A low moan came from the darkness.

He pushed the torch forward and carefully pulled away the rubble that blocked his way. With one more wriggle he was beside Madame Carrière. Now he could see the great wooden beam that was protecting her and at the same time crushing the life out of her. She was caught with the beam across her shoulders. Her feet and legs were trapped in a tangle of timbers. She strained to keep the beam in its place, but as she weakened Jamie could hear the creaking and grinding of the stones in the wall above.

Fragments of debris rained down through the cracks. He pushed one stone into place beneath the beam. Now he needed another on top of the first. He stuck the torch into a crevice. With both hands free, he pulled a large boulder until he held it tightly to his chest. He slowly rolled over onto his back, still holding the stone, which was then on top of him. He pushed up with all his strength, lifting the stone until he could slide it into place on top of the first.

"Madame, if you can push hard enough to raise the beam a little, then I can get a support underneath. Madame, can you hear me?"

She didn't answer, but Jamie saw her back straining against the beam. It began to move. As it shifted, the debris above fell faster. Jamie braced his feet and pushed his stone with one great effort before his heels slipped and he fell back. With stone chips, dust, and pieces of mortar raining down on his head, he waited for the crushing pain of the house collapsing on him. A minute passed and then another. The beam was holding! He turned over on his stomach and twisted his head to where he could inspect it. The beam was resting on the pillar he had built.

"Madame, we did it," he shouted. "Madame?" He moved the torch so that he could see her face.

He touched her cheek. It was covered with grey dust caked with sweat. There was no sign of life. "Madame?"

He felt panic rising. Then her eyes opened. She smiled at him, and he started to cry. He felt happy and foolish at the same time.

"Go and get some help, little fishman," she whispered.

Jamie called back to Heli, "The beam's propped up, but you'll have to keep the stones above us from moving when you take away the others."

Jamie stayed with Madame Carrière and shouted warnings to Heli when the creaking above him became too ominous. Most of the time he lay with his eyes closed, reciting a poem that Angus had taught him when they were in the hold of the press-gang transport.

> God shield the house, the fire, the kine,
> Every one who dwells herein tonight.
> Shield myself and my beloved group,
> Preserve us from violence and from harm;
> Preserve us from foes this night...

The lilting words stopped him thinking about what would happen if the beam broke.

After two hours that seemed like two weeks, the rescuers were able to pull Madame Carrière and Jamie to safety. They were set down gently in the street. Side by side, covered in dust and streaked with blood, they looked like corpses.

As he lay enjoying the freedom of the open air, Jamie saw Heli kneel beside Madame Carrière, and gently wash her face.

"It was so strange in there, Heli," she whispered. "I think I even went a bit mad once. I could hear Jacques praying but I couldn't understand any of the words."

Jamie felt guilty when he realized that Angus's poem was in Gaelic. There seemed to be no point in trying to explain. Madame was as happy as he was just to be alive.

The bombs had stopped, and the people went back to their cellars to wait for daylight. Jeanne treated Jamie like a hero, washing his wounds. She grew quite indignant when he said that he shouldn't come into the house because of his fishy smell.

Sleat stood on the shore of Île d'Orléans gazing at Quebec. "We've gone to enough trouble to get here," he said to Sinn, "and it looks like a promising place to end my quest. What have you learned about the old fox and his cub?"

"Duncan is with the army, but he hasn't used his own name. He has vanished from sight as completely as ever. With thousands of troops constantly on the move, we will only find him by luck. The boy is with the French. The navy thinks he is a deserter and if he is found he will be hanged."

Sleat looked puzzled. "That's ridiculous. We can't have the navy hanging him before we have found his father. But they could be helped to capture him. A trial could flush Macpherson from cover. See what you can do about that, Sinn. Where is the boy?"

"He was captured and taken to Quebec. That's all I know. They're fighting a war here. I can't just bribe someone to row over to Quebec and ask if they have any British deserters walking about."

"Then go yourself," said Sleat.

10
The Growing Menace
August 1759

In the morning the residents of Lower Town crept out from their cellars to search for missing relatives and survey the damage from the attack. They learned that Upper Town had suffered even more. The Ursuline Convent had been struck several times and only the valiant efforts of the nuns had saved it from being destroyed by fire.

"The war has finally arrived," Heli said to Jeanne and Jamie over the thin gruel that passed for their breakfast. "The next barrage will be worse, and we won't just get the bombs that fall short of Upper Town. They'll turn Lower Town to ashes. Jeanne, you are to go to your uncle in Trois Rivières. It's a long journey and dangerous, but it will be safer than staying here. Jamie, I want you to go with her, not as a *prisoner* but as a friend. She has a mind of her own, this girl, but will forgive an old man for being worried about his favourite child."

"If you stay, I stay," said Jeanne. Her face was set in the mulish expression that Jamie had learned to recognize. "I won't leave you. Not for a thousand British bombs."

"Child, child, the journey would kill me, and if I have to die I want to do it here. I won't insist that you leave today, but you must go soon. Try to understand what it means to me. You are all that I have left in the world, I must know that you are safe." Heli blew his nose vigorously in a large red handkerchief and tried to smile. "Now find some food or starvation will get us before the bombs do."

"I won't try to persuade you one way or the other," said Jamie as they walked through the rubble, "but if you go, I'll go with you."

She hesitated, "I can't leave him. He's all the family I have. I know what he means, but I'll wait and hope he's wrong. Maybe it won't be as bad as he thinks."

So they stayed, but Heli was right. All during that hot and rainy August, the barrages grew worse. Each night the bombs arced across the river, like deadly fireflies dancing through the darkness. Scarcely a building was left standing. The Bishop's Palace lay in ruins, the cathedral was a burnt-out shell with only part of a tower and blackened stonework left. Upper Town was destroyed and Lower Town was reduced to ashes. The threatened city was almost empty. The remaining men of the town had been formed into companies—one for guard duty, another to put out the fires that raged on all sides from the hail of British bombs. Most of the women and children had left, climbing Palace Hill and then on through the great gates to the countryside. The General Hospital which was north of the town, beyond the range of the British guns, was filled with the sick and wounded.

Heli alternately threatened and begged but Jeanne wouldn't leave, although their house had been levelled too, and they had to sleep and live in the vaulted cellar. Even Madame Carrière had departed but that was only after her three sons arrived from the country, tied her to her fish barrow and wheeled her off, as she shouted, "I wish all the hairs on my head were dragons to fight them." They offered to take Jeanne the same way, but she ran away and hid until they had gone.

Each morning Jeanne and Jamie would emerge from the cellar to search for food. There was no more bread to be had. All the ovens in town had stopped baking, and everyone had to eat biscuits while they waited for new ovens to be built on the outskirts.

One day in early September, Jeanne decided that they should go up beyond the gates to hunt for raspberries. Rubble blocked the empty streets. Whole sides were torn out of the roofless houses—here a broken rocker abandoned in a corner, there a pot shattered by a cannon ball. From the smouldering ruins of one house, Jeanne rescued a scorched rag doll. She shuddered as they passed the gibbet that had been erected opposite the terrace of the Chateau St. Louis to discourage thieves from ransacking the abandoned houses after dark.

Now and then a head would pop out of a cellar and call a mournful greeting. The only other signs of life were the starveling dogs prowling about in the devastation and the workmen putting out fires.

It was a relief to reach the plains beyond the gates, to escape the pall of smoke that hung over the city night and day. They were too late to find many raspberries. "Other people have been here first," Jeanne said, surveying her near-empty basket, but she did come across a patch of mushrooms, which cheered her.

They rambled around the green fields until late afternoon, happy to be away from the grim scenes behind them, then sat down in the shade of an elm on the heights overlooking the river.

"How much longer can the British keep their soldiers here?" asked Jamie, making a face as he bit into a withered raspberry.

"Some say one month, others less. The last ship for the year usually leaves in October, but there are many soldiers to take away."

"Then they'll try something soon."

"Haven't they done enough now?" Jeanne's thin cheeks were flushed. "They've destroyed the farms on the river, burned Baie Saint Paul, and bombarded the city. But I told you, they can't take Quebec."

"The French said the British couldn't navigate the river—well there they are. They weren't supposed to be able to bomb and mortar the town from the south shore—look around you. They couldn't sail under the guns of Quebec to get up river, now they have ships off

Cap Rouge and all the supplies to Quebec have to run the gauntlet. How can you stay so sure that they can't attack the town?"

"Because I have to believe it," Jeanne said quietly.

"I'm sorry," said Jamie. "I never know when to stop. My father tried to teach me to think before I talk, but it's a hard lesson to learn."

"You want to find your father, and I don't want to lose my grandfather. Perhaps we both need the English to leave. Then you can go to Virginia. You said he'd meet you there."

"It's a long way. I thought that a great distance was one that took all day to walk, until I sailed across the ocean. Then when we reached the St. Lawrence I discovered that a river could seem longer still. But I've come this far, so what's a few more miles." Jamie scrambled to his feet and picked up his basket. "Let's go back. It looks so peaceful down there, maybe we'll have a quiet night."

The bombardment of the town began at sunset. Very early next morning Jamie left the cellar to see how much more destruction had taken place. On his way up Palace Hill, he saw an old man sitting with his back to a half-demolished wall. His black hat was slouched over his face to keep the first rays of the sun out of his eyes as he puffed contentedly on a short clay pipe. Jamie called out a greeting, and the old man waved.

When he reached the top he spoke to one of the sentries at the gate.

"What's the news? Did any food come down the river last night?"

"Not for you," snapped the sentry. "Why don't you go to the woods like everybody else? We don't have enough food for the soldiers. Look over there," he said, pointing toward Beauport. "These troops have been at their stations all night with the British fleet trying to make a landing. There's a lot of empty bellies in that crowd."

"Leave him be," said the other sentry. "He's Heli's boy. Try the convent. I saw two sisters there when we came on duty. You might get a bite to eat from them."

As Jamie approached the ruins of the convent, he saw an excited crowd heading for the fort. He caught up with a man at the back of the group. "What's happening?"

The man was panting, trying to keep up with the others, and could barely gasp the words. "The British are here."

"Where?" said Jamie, looking around as he stumbled along beside him.

The man pointed wildly. "Above the town."

Jamie ran ahead to get more news, but all the answers were different. The crowd was growing now as they approached the walls of the town. A dreadful chorus of sobs and prayers filled the air. Jamie pushed his way through until he reached the wall and could see the fields beyond. In the distance a line of British troops stretched across the plain as far as he could see. He squirmed back through the terrified crowd and raced toward Lower Town. All along the way people asked, "Is it true?" The town was in a panic.

He skidded his way back down Palace Hill, shouting to the old man who was still sunning himself by the wall, "The British are here." The old man jumped up and scuttled away. "That even got him to move," Jamie thought.

He burst into the cellar too breathless to talk. Heli and Jeanne waited anxiously until he finally blurted out the news.

Jeanne sat silent with tears trickling down her cheeks. Heli spoke first, "Well, children, it will soon be over. Go to the General Hospital. The good sisters will need all the help they can get when the fighting begins. I have enough food for a week, and by then we will have won the battle for Quebec." He dried Jeanne's tears with his handkerchief. "Take care of each other," he said as he ushered them out into the daylight.

Jeanne smiled at him. "You take care and don't forget to feed the cat."

"We're an odd pair of allies," she said to Jamie as they trudged toward the hill.

"When I was sailing up the river, my friend George asked what I'd do if I had to fight the French. He knew that I'd spent most of my life being hunted by the English. I told him that I'd look after the wounded, French and English. So perhaps we aren't such an odd pair after all."

When they reached Upper Town, Jamie started to walk quickly, then he stopped. "Sit down for a minute."

Startled, Jeanne obeyed. "Who are you looking for?" He was staring back, studying the milling crowd of soldiers and townspeople.

"I don't know, but I have a feeling that we're being

followed. When I travelled with my father in France, we used to play a game. First he'd follow me and I'd have to try to lose him. Then I had to follow him without losing him. I thought it was a strange game, but now I know that he was training me to survive with him as a hunted man. And I have that feeling again. I'm sure someone is following us. Let's see how good he is. You go down the alley and hide in the first doorway. Watch the street, but don't let anyone who passes see you. Watch everyone who passes the alley until you count to twenty. Then go round the back way to the Turcotte house. I'll wait at the corner there and we'll do the same thing again. If I'm right you'll see one of the people again, and that's the one who is after me. You follow whoever you suspect until they stop trailing me. We'll meet at the General Hospital."

Jeanne looked at the people hurrying past and wondered how she was supposed to remember all these faces. Then she jumped up, glared at Jamie, and slapped his face. "Run away if you like," she shouted. As he stood, bewildered, she whispered, "Just playing my part, idiot," and swept off down the alley.

Jamie stared after her until she vanished into a doorway, then shook himself out of his surprise. Rubbing his smarting cheek, he started to walk in the direction of the General Hospital. When he reached the Turcotte house he slumped down beside the doorway and gnawed on a biscuit. Once he felt Jeanne had had enough time to catch up, he got to his feet and walked on.

The way to the St. Jean gate was blocked with soldiers. They had marched across the bridge of boats from the

Beauport shore to the plains above Quebec to challenge the English invader. Along with the soldiers Jamie squeezed his way through the crowd of cheering townsfolk and on through the gate in the town wall. It was hard to believe that only yesterday he and Jeanne had been hunting for raspberries on the Plains of Abraham. Now two armies were preparing for battle there.

When he reached the great stone quadrangle of the hospital, he went inside to a dark, cool silence. The sisters moved quickly among the wounded from the bombings, preparing for the onslaught of wounded from the battle which could come at any time. Every building at the convent was filled with the homeless and the helpless: the dining-rooms and dormitories, the stables and barns, the garrets and halls for the sick. Even the church had been turned into a hospital ward. The nuns from the Hotel Dieu and the Ursulines were there too. Jamie found his friend, Sister Luc, and she immediately put him to work.

When Jeanne arrived, he was carrying buckets of water to refill all the basins he could find. "I'm sorry," he said. "Maybe I sent you on a wild goose chase."

She turned over an empty bucket and sat down. "Not a wild goose chase," she said breathlessly, "but just as tiring. An old man with a black hat was following you. When you reached the hospital he turned back. He would have seen me but just then there were shots from the heights, and he looked up." She shuddered. "I've never seen such pale eyes. I didn't give them a second chance to see me, I can tell you."

"Come now, you two," said Sister Luc, rustling along

the long corridor. "There is work to be done and no time for gossip."

"Sinn," said Jamie.

Sister Luc gave him a surprised look before hurrying on to her next task.

"It's a man called Sinn," Jamie explained. "He works for Sleat who wants to kill my father. That means that somehow they must have followed me to Quebec, but they would only follow me if they felt that I could lead them to my father. Does that mean that my father has found out that I was press-ganged and that he's here? In Quebec?" In the midst of the despair around him he felt a surge of hope.

Jeanne stood up and handed Jamie the bucket. "You'd better work while you think, or Sister Luc will be after you as well."

Jamie smiled. "Well, at least she's real, not part of this world of disguise where no one is who they seem to be—including me."

New rumours arrived with each group who sought refuge in the convent. Then the wounded began to arrive. There was no longer any doubt. The battle had begun.

"Water!" Jamie picked up his buckets and ran along the corridor.

The stream of wounded was now a torrent of dead and dying soldiers. Before anyone could pause long enough to ask how the battle was going, word came that it was over. The French had left the battlefield in disarray. Only the Canadian militia were delaying the advance of the British army.

General Wolfe was dead, the wounded soldiers reported, but the English had won. Montcalm was dead or dying...the French army had been destroyed...was escaping across the St. Charles River to regroup and fight again...no one knew what to believe.

The doors of the General Hospital were barred and the sisters waited for the arrival of the victors. In the shadowed wards the wounded were already beyond the reach of war.

"Over here!" Jamie brought water to the terrified drummer boy with the sabre wound on his cheek. "They're coming! The English devils." He sank back onto his pillow and covered his face.

"Be calm, my son," soothed the tiny nun by his side, but Jamie saw that her eyes reflected his terror.

Night came. As Jamie passed the door of the chapel, he saw the sisters from all three convents prostrate at the foot of the altar. In white robes and black, their veils covered their shoulders as they prayed before the great crucifix. There was silence except for the sputtering of the candles in the tall silver sconces. It was as if the entire convent was holding its breath. Jamie stood at the back in the shadows. He heard a rustling noise beside him and turned to see Jeanne sink to her knees, with her eyes fixed on the altar.

Knock! Knock! Knock!

The sound broke the silence like shots.

The prostrate figures lay like dead moths in the candlelight and continued their wordless prayers.

The rapping grew louder, more impatient. Two young

nuns, not much older than Jeanne, left to open the heavy door.

A British officer stood in the doorway with a squad of kilted soldiers behind him. Jamie saw the look of pity on his face at the sight of the trembling girls.

"Where is your Mother Superior?" he asked gently.

Wordlessly, they pointed toward the chapel. The stately figure of Mother de Sainte Claude emerged and walked slowly toward the officer.

"Do not be afraid," he said. "We will not harm you or the sisters. But part of our army must surround your house. It is possible that the French army may return and attack us, but your hospital will remain under our protection.

The Mother Superior inclined her head in agreement and the officer ordered his men into their positions. Jamie heard a strange sound beside him and turned to see what it was. Jeanne was weeping!

The arrival of the British changed little in the hospital. Everyone continued to tend the wounded and attempt to comfort the dying, only now the wounded and dying were from both armies.

There was no time to worry about Sinn or Sleat. Jeanne and Jamie worked until they were exhausted, slept briefly, and then worked again. The next three days passed in a haze of suffering. The remnant of the French army was retreating to Trois Rivières; the defence of Quebec depended on the strength of the fortifications and the garrison inside. Jamie asked Sister Luc whether she thought the walls of the city could withstand a siege.

"It is starvation not cannon that threatens our people," she said sombrely. "There is no food."

On the fourth day word came that the Chevalier de Ramezay had surrendered Quebec.

Jeanne and Jamie had finished their work and were resting in a corner of the main ward when they heard the news. Jeanne sat, white-faced and still, while slow tears rolled down her cheeks. Jamie didn't know how to console her. He wasn't quite sure how he felt himself.

She shuddered, then sat up and flicked away the tears with her sleeves. "No more crying now." She smiled, although her lips quivered. "I should go back to see my grandfather. What will you do now, Jacques?"

"I have to find out whether the navy wants to welcome me or hang me. My enemies are here with Sinn, but perhaps some of my friends are here too. I told you about Willie the Ferret and Angus the Piper. I'll look for them first. Angus should be easy to find. How many giant pipers can the army have?"

"And your father?"

"I could never hope to find him. He'll have to find me, but I have to make that possible. No one would look for me here."

"Except Sinn. *He* knows where you are."

Jamie sat up with a jolt. "How could I forget that?" he groaned. "He's probably just biding his time, an eagle lazily circling above a rabbit."

"We could leave tonight, and you can stay with us until you think of what to do next," Jeanne suggested. "Sister Luc can spare us. There will be more people to help now that the town has...surrendered."

A small boy came out of the darkness into the pool of light cast by their candle. " Sister Luc is looking for you." He tugged at Jamie's sleeve.

"Where is she?"

"Over there," the child said, pointing into the shadows. "By the side door."

"I'll tell her that we want to leave tonight," Jamie said, rolling up his pack. "Collect your things." He picked his way across the dark room, moving from one pool of candlelight to another, avoiding the sleeping figures curled up on the floor with their forlorn bundles beside them. He saw the nun's robes silhouetted against the open door as she looked out at the night sky.

"Sister Luc, we'd like to leave tonight, but we'll come back if you need us." He spoke in a low voice, not wanting to disturb the patients.

The black habit turned and a strong thin hand gripped him by the neck. "But I need you *now*," whispered Sinn.

From across the room Jeanne saw a swirl of black and Jamie vanished into the night.

Sinn hurled Jamie out the door, into the grasp of Sleat's men waiting in the darkness.

"Precious cargo," Sinn hissed as one of them knocked Jamie unconscious. "Handle it with care or I'll offer you to his father."

Jamie was carried quickly to Upper Town where Sleat had already taken over a merchant's house. It stood on the edge of the cliff looking out over the river. One end had fallen into the town below when part of the cliff crumbled during the bombing. The men were afraid of the house, sure that the rest of it would fall over the cliff too, burying them under its rubble. Sleat enjoyed their fear and made them sleep in the rooms where doors that once led to other rooms now opened into midair. "Hanging doors," he called them, "with a drop fit for a king."

"We have the bait for your trap," Sinn announced as they entered the room and set Jamie on the floor in front of Sleat.

"How do you plan to set it?"

"I want him handed over to the Princess Amelia. The Captain will set up a court martial. Put posters up around the town. I want it to be talked about everywhere. His father will try to rescue him, and all we have to do is watch, wait, and be ready to strike. This time there must be no mistake." Sleat's face shone with hate.

11

Baiting the Trap

September 1759

Before Jeanne could cross the room to follow, a gentle hand touched her shoulder.

"Where are you going, my child?"

She looked up into Sister Luc's careworn face.

"Sister! How can you be here when you just went outside with Jacques?"

"What are you talking about? I haven't seen him since the two of you finished your work for the night."

Jeanne stared at the empty doorway and back at Sister Luc. "You didn't send him a message?"

"No."

Jeanne ran to the door and out into the night. "Jacques?" she cried but there was no answer. "Where are you?" She stumbled over a bundle that lay on the ground just beside the step and picked it up. It was his pack!

Sister Luc caught up with her. "What is it, my child?"

"Jacques' enemies have got him," she babbled, clutching the pack. "I have to find his friends and tell them."

"I do not understand you," Sister Luc said, "but I do know that you will not find anyone out there tonight. Except perhaps a British patrol who will shoot anything that moves in the darkness. Come back inside and tell me what this is about, then I will help you find whoever you want to find when daylight comes."

Reluctantly, Jeanne followed the nun back into the hospital. She told her about Jamie, about his friends and enemies, and about his father. "Sleat's got him, I know he has. He..." Exhausted, she fell asleep in mid-sentence.

Sister Luc awoke her soon after sunrise. "I have talked with the British wounded. I think I can tell you where to find the giant piper."

"Where?" Jeanne jumped to her feet, ready to leave immediately.

"He is with the soldiers camped just outside the St. Louis Gate. Highlanders. You will recognize them by their kilts. Like that one over there." She pointed to a small man, swathed in bandages, who was loudly demanding breakfast. "I have made you a package of food to take to your grandfather after you have found the piper."

Jeanne thanked Sister Luc and set off at once. The devastated streets were no longer empty. Gradually the people of Quebec were straggling back, returning to their fallen city. But there were redcoats, not white, manning the gates and guarding the entrance to the Intendant's Palace.

"I'll think about that later," Jeanne said, swallowing hard at the sight of the union flag snapping in the breeze.

She went through the gate, beyond the walls of the city and cautiously approached the rows of tents with the cooking fires already smoking. Except for Jamie and George, she had never spoken to anyone British in her life, and she wasn't sure how to start a conversation with the enemy.

A soldier, stirring a pot over the fire, looked up. "Sorry, young miss," he said in halting French. "Strict orders. No civilians permitted near the camp."

"I have to talk to a piper called Angus about a friend of his. It's important."

"Well, that's different. Any friend of Angus is welcome. Have some breakfast, and I'll call him." He handed her a plate of porridge and a large horn spoon and strolled off along the line of tents.

He was soon back with the biggest man Jeanne had ever seen.

She gazed up into his face. "You're just as Jacques said. A giant."

Angus looked down at her, perplexed. "Jacques?"

"Your friend from Scotland...from Normandy. You were press-ganged together."

Angus roared with laughter and delight. "Jamie. You found the little rogue?" He sat down and listened attentively while in between spoonfuls of porridge Jeanne told him about Jamie's capture on Île aux Coudres, how he had been her prisoner, and all that led up to his disappearance from the hospital.

When she finished, he sighed and scratched his sunburnt ear. "Left to me, I would be storming into that devil Sleat's prison to rescue the boy, but Sleat is more cunning than me and I would never be succeeding. We are needing Willie the Ferret. Someone with the craftiness to match Sleat and beat him at his own game."

"Where is Willie?"

"Now that's a problem," said Angus, scratching the other ear. "He is in the King's navy, and we don't know where, do we? And if we did know where, they wouldn't be letting us have him. Would they?"

"Who wouldn't?" asked Jeanne. The porridge had heartened her even if she was in the midst of the enemy tents—and it was hard to think of this beaming mountain of a man as an enemy.

"Why the admiral, of course."

"I could ask him," remembering George. "I know the admiral's nephew."

"Do you then? Well that might do something. Wait here and I'll just be telling the captain that I have to help a Macpherson."

"This captain will let you come just because Jacques is a Macpherson?" Jeanne couldn't think of him as Jamie.

"Well then, but isn't he being a Macpherson himself?" said Angus.

Jeanne was puzzled by the words, but understood the meaning. "Can we trust him to know about Jacques' father?"

Angus became indignant. "Trust? I'd leave my pipes in that man's care. What is there to tell him about Jamie's father?"

Jeanne explained that Jamie thought his father must be near, or why would Sleat go to so much trouble to follow a boy? And the only way he could be here, and hidden from Sleat, would be if he were in the army, one man among thousands and using another name.

"If that is so," said Angus, "he'll be with Highlanders. And if I can't get word to a Highlander among Highlanders, then may I never be seeing Skye again." He urged more porridge upon her and disappeared among the tents.

He was soon back, ready to take Jeanne to find the admiral. "It's all settled. If he's here we will get the word to him. I even promised to be playing the pipes at the captain's wedding if he finds Jamie's father for us."

They walked past the charred remains of Upper Town and down the hill to the ruined buildings on Champlain Street, where the neighbours were already hard at work, clearing away piles of stones and tearing down broken walls.

Jeanne walked more and more slowly as they came closer to Heli's house. She didn't want Angus to see that she was afraid.

She stopped, so suddenly that he almost marched over her. Something small and red and furry was twining round her ankles, purring loudly. "Minette!" She scooped the little cat up in her arms and stepped over the battered threshold. She knelt beside the sagging floorboards, all that remained of the house, and stared down into the cellar. She tried to find a brave voice to call "Grandfather" but it came out as a sob. Silence. Then, from across the street, she heard his voice: "Jeanne. Over here."

She ran into his arms.

"What a day." he beamed. "No tears now, my child." He smoothed her hair. "First Madame Carrière comes home from the country, and now you arrive. It's just like old times."

Madame sat in the shade of what remained of the wall of her house, with a plank balanced on the rubble and a crust of bread carefully set out on it. Jeanne rushed across and hugged her too, then remembered Angus and went back for him.

"A friend of Jacques' you say," said Madame Carrière. "That's all we need to know. Sit down, young man, and share our dinner." She looked at the crust of bread and laughed ruefully. "I forgot for a moment that we are not able to offer much these days."

"Sister Luc gave me this." Jeanne presented her package.

After they had eaten, while Jeanne described Jamie's disappearance, Angus heaved aside enough stones and timbers to make it easier for Madame Carrière to get into her cellar.

"Now that I know you're safe, I have to find help," said Jeanne. "Where do I look for an admiral?"

"On a ship with a special flag," Angus replied. "All you need do is speak to the sailors at the wharf. They'll be so surprised at the question that they'll be pointing it out to you."

Jeanne and Angus soon reached the wharf and studied the flags on the ships anchored in the river. "It might be that one," said Angus, wishing that he had paid more attention when he was in the navy.

They walked on to where four sailors were sunning themselves. A longboat rocked gently in the water below.

"This young lady wants to know which is the admiral's ship."

"You hear that, mates?" The sailor grinned and pointed at Angus's kilt. "These two ladies want to see the admiral."

Without a word, Angus reached down, picked him up and threw him clear across the longboat into the river.

"Now then laddie," he said to the next sailor, "were you hearing the question?"

"Over there," the sailor said hastily. "Sir."

"Is the admiral on board?"

"No, sir, 'e's ashore. We're waitin' to take 'im back. Sir."

Angus sat down beside the now-respectful men and motioned to Jeanne to join him. He translated what had been said, then turned back to the sailor. "Are any of you knowing Willie the Ferret?"

He shook his head and reached over to give a hand to his spluttering mate who was climbing back out of the river.

"Do you know Willie the Ferret?"

The sailor looked hunted. "Will he throw me in again, if I say I do?"

"Here, man," said Angus. "Have a drop of this. It will

be taking the cold out of your system." He produced a flask from his pocket. "Just don't be insulting the kilt, that's all."

The dripping sailor took a swig from the flask and gave a strangled gasp. "That's liquid fire," he choked.

"Water of Life," said Angus proudly. "Now, do you know Willie or not?"

"I've heard of him," the man said carefully.

"Where is he then?"

The sailor pointed to a small ship riding at anchor beyond the *Princess Amelia*.

"Oh, poor Willie," said Angus. "On such a little ship. We have to get him off that, Jeanne. A man couldn't be breathing on a ship that size."

Suddenly the sailors jumped to their feet and stood at attention. Angus was quick to do the same. Jeanne did not understand what was happening. Then she heard brisk footsteps behind her and whirled round.

"The admiral," Angus whispered.

A majestic figure strode toward her, looking more imposing than the governor himself. Remembering her manners, Jeanne stepped forward and curtsied. "Sir, I have news of your nephew."

He stopped in mid-stride, and she wondered if he spoke French. The Highlanders all seemed to, but he was English.

To her relief, he answered in French. "Come aboard and tell me about him while we prepare to sail." He looked up at Angus. "I remember you from Halifax. Are you her escort?"

"Yes, sir."

"Wait here, and I'll send her back when we've talked. You never did like the water, did you?"

"No, sir. Thank you, sir," said Angus, looking relieved.

The sailors handed Jeanne down into the longboat, and when they arrived at the side of the ship, the dry sailor motioned for her to climb on his back and carried her up the rope ladder.

The admiral led her below to the Great Cabin. Jeanne tried not to be overawed by the massive wooden table, the silver candlesticks, and the rows of broad-based decanters glinting on the sideboard.

The admiral sat down on an armchair and motioned her to another.

"Now, mademoiselle, tell me what you can of my nephew. I have been trying to get him exchanged, but I have had no word from the rapscallion himself since his capture."

So George had forgotten to write. Or perhaps his message had been lost. Jeanne told the admiral about meeting the lonely boy on the ramparts, and how they had talked together before he and the other midshipmen had been sent to Trois Rivières. "Jacques...Jamie was my prisoner. He promised not to run away on his father's honour. And now he's been captured by his enemies, and we need this Willie the Ferret to help rescue him."

The admiral listened so intently that she forgot her nervousness. "He's not a traitor at all. What was he to do?"

"It's a strange request, but war produces strange

requests," the admiral said. He went to his desk, searched among the papers piled on top, and picked one up. He read it, frowning. "Your friend Jamie is wanted as a deserter or a spy. Both charges have been laid against him." He sat down at the table and drummed his fingers on the shining wood. Jeanne held her breath. The admiral smiled at her anxious face. "I'll send Willie back with you because I'm grateful for news of my nephew, and because I remember Jamie as a good friend to George. But your Jamie will have to face a court martial, and I will not interfere with the justice of that court."

He gave crisp instructions to a spruce young lieutenant, and soon Jeanne was being rowed over to the small ship to pick up a very surprised Willie and take him ashore for a reunion with an even more surprised Angus.

"You're a sight for sore eyes," said Willie when they met. "Maybe you can tell me what this young one has been trying to get through my tin ear on the way here. I was never one for foreign languages."

Angus told what he knew of Jamie's plight as Jeanne led them back to Champlain Street. When Willie came in, Minette, who had been curled up on the scorched remains of a rag rug, arched her back and hissed. Heli greeted his visitors. "Your friend has a strange effect on cats," he said to Angus. Minette was now crouched in the far corner of the cellar. Her fur stood on end and low bloodcurdling sounds rumbled from the back of her throat.

"Don't carry on so." Willie soothed the irate cat, then set her outside on what was left of the doorstep. After she stalked across the road, still growling softly, he reached deep into one of his pockets and produced—Fergie. From another pocket he pulled out a small ham, cheese, ship's biscuit, and a bottle of brandy and set them on the large slab of rock that Heli was using as a table.

"A magician," said the fortune teller.

"I always travel prepared. You never know when you might get your next meal."

Jeanne was delighted when she discovered that the strange little beast was friendly, and she followed Fergie around the cellar as he explored every corner.

After they had eaten, they arranged to meet next morning at the St. Louis Gate.

"Remember," said Willie, "that Sinn has a great curiosity. He might decide to find out what Jamie's friend here is doing about his disappearance. We can't afford to let him discover that she has found allies." Jeanne felt encouraged by his black-toothed grin. "Just sit by the gate until I come. Angus will wait in the camp for us."

Next morning she took her basket and climbed to Upper Town. She gradually made her way to the St. Louis Gate where she sat in the shade to rest. Almost at once, Willie appeared and in badly broken French asked her to take him to Angus.

They found him sitting glumly at a fire.

"No word to speak of," he said dolefully. "Charlie Macdonald spread the word among the Highlanders on the plain, and then went over to the Lévis shore. He sent Andrew Cameron back to tell us that he'd had no luck yet, but that he was going on to the next camp. Here is

Andrew now." He pointed to a soldier bringing wood for the fire.

"Well, I have news but you won't like it," said Willie, pausing to light his pipe from the fire. Then he produced a poster from his pocket. "I tore this off a door. They're all over the town."

"What does it say?" Jeanne asked.

Angus laughed, "I am not reading English and Willie is not speaking French. Andrew, you look as though you're reading what it says. Are you just pretending like me or can you tell us, in French, so that Jeanne can understand?"

The soldier set down his wood and took the poster. "It is a notice of the court martial of Jamie Macpherson, a British sailor who deserted in time of war. He will be tried and, if found guilty, will be hanged."

Everyone was suddenly silent.

"It's their usual way of reminding us that desertion is not the way to escape being killed in battle," continued Cameron. His voice was bleak.

"It's more than that," said Willie. "It's bait in the trap. The navy wouldn't bother so much with a loblolly boy. Sleat has made those posters. He knows that when Duncan Macpherson sees them he will try to rescue Jamie. And Sleat will be waiting."

He lifted Fergie out of his pocket and stroked his fur. The ferret blinked in the sunlight. Willie muttered a few words of Glaswegian which none of the others could follow and pointed to Andrew. Fergie lay still for a moment, then ran over to Andrew Cameron, crawled up on his shoulder, and began to nibble his ear.

"I had a feeling it was you," said Willie, "but I wanted Fergie to prove it. He'll not be fooled by changing the colour of the hair, the shape of the nose, and even the height of a man. Duncan, I have never understood how you can change your height."

Angus looked bewildered.

Cameron reached over and shook Willie's hand warmly. "I couldn't ask for better company in hard times. I had to be sure that we were among friends."

He turned to Angus and Jeanne. "You must forgive me for not telling you sooner that I am Duncan Macpherson. Jamie may have told you that I am slow to trust strangers. It keeps me alive," he added with a smile.

"Now," his smile faded. "How are we to rescue Jamie?"

"Sleat can't be sure how long it will take you to see or hear about the trial," said Willie. "Jamie will be taken to the *Princess Amelia* for the court martial. Sleat will expect you to sniff around the trap and won't do anything to scare you off. The navy will do the guarding of the prisoner for him. Sleat will watch and wait."

Angus translated for Jeanne as Willie thought aloud.

"Willie, you find Sleat," said Duncan. "You know his ways. He has set his trap and baited it, maybe he will be so intent on watching the trap that he will forget to watch himself. There's a tavern back in business in Lower Town, The Three Pigeons. I'll meet you there after dark. Bring Angus."

He was gone before Jeanne could ask what she could do. She turned around to ask Willie, but he was halfway to the St. Louis gate. "Angus, don't you disappear before you tell me how I can help. Will they really hang him?"

"Don't even be thinking about that." The smile on his freckled face was so comforting that it was hard for her to believe that Jamie's troubles could last.

"We'll get word to you at your grandfather's house as soon as there is news."

Sleat paced up and down the room in a rage. "What the devil do you mean? They can't hold the trial tomorrow. Crean was told that I needed a week to be sure the boy's father would hear of his trial. The fools will probably find the boy guilty and hang him the same day. Bring Crean to me and I'll tell him when he can hold his trial. The boy belongs to me, not the British navy."

"The admiral sent orders that the trial be held tomorrow, and what's worse, he made it clear that it had better be a fair trial or someone would answer to him," said Sinn from the corner of the room.

"Someday you'll try my patience too far, Sinn. Why didn't you warn me about this? Isn't that what I pay you for?"

"You said I worried too much about the boy, and if I talked to you again about him you'd cut my tongue out," said Sinn with careful innocence.

"Get out," shouted Sleat. "All of you. Out. I want that boy watched every minute. I want Duncan Macpherson caught, and we may only have tonight to do it."

All but his two bodyguards started to leave.

"You two as well. This may be my last chance to catch Macpherson. It must not fail."

149

12
The Meeting
September 1759

Willie sat puffing on his pipe with a mug of cider in front of him, surveying the boisterous, crowded tavern. He had found a spot where he could watch the door and was speculating on whether he would recognize Duncan Macpherson when he arrived. Willie had his back to the only wall in the place which looked as though it could stand on its own. The rest of the walls were braced with timbers; the roof was a makeshift cover which dripped rain on the patrons below. No one seemed to mind. They were sailors ashore, or soldiers on a pass, and they had all been in worse places in their time. The Three Pigeons was already packed, filled with smoke and song. Each newcomer had to squeeze his way in the door and from there to the bar.

As Willie drank his cider and waited, a sailor carrying four mugs in one hand above his head used the other hand to pry his way through the crowd. He limped toward Willie and squeezed onto the bench beside him.

"Crowded as The Black Bull," he remarked casually while taking a long draft from the first mug.

Willie let Fergie pop his head out of a pocket. "Well, Fergie, do we know the company?" The ferret sniffed the sailor's hand and squeaked happily.

Duncan put down the first mug with a sigh of satisfaction and picked up the next.

"I was trying to decide whether you'd come through the door or leak in through the roof with the rain," said Willie. "But I missed on both counts. I'm glad to see you've joined the navy. A superior service."

"Did you find Sleat?" Duncan asked the question lightly, but Willie knew his old friend was worried.

"That wasn't hard, but getting to him will be. He's taken over a house on the rock above Lower Town. Half the place has fallen over the cliff, and the other half looks as though it might follow at any minute. His men guard it like a small fortress, but I hear that they are scared to death staying there. Do you remember that house in Glasgow, where the half of it was demolished when the gunpowder that the Jacobites were storing there blew up?" Duncan nodded. "It's just like that, with the upstairs door opening into space. Only this one is at the edge of the cliff."

"Could I get up to that door? It might be a way to pay Sleat a surprise visit."

"Not from the cliffside," Willie closed his eyes to try to picture the house, "but if you could reach the roof, you might be able to lower yourself by a rope. Sleat makes the men sleep up there. He won't let them block the door because he knows they are afraid the house will fall over the cliff, and he enjoys their fear."

"We have to go to the fortune teller to meet Angus. We'll ask him for rope," said Willie. "Just let me help you with that ale and we'll be on our way."

When they reached Champlain Street they checked that the house was not being watched, and then entered the cellar where Angus was entertaining Jeanne and Heli with tales of Skye. Heli found them a length of strong rope when they had explained what they needed, and Jeanne persuaded them that she should come too.

When they reached the house in Upper Town, they watched it from the shelter of a bombed-out building opposite. Candles burned on the ground floor and shadows moved back and forth across the window.

"We must find out how many are in there, and whether Sleat is with them," said Duncan.

Before he could say more, Jeanne ran across the street. She pulled herself up to the window and peered in. She was back in a moment. "Sinn is there with five men. There's someone dressed like a gentleman who is shouting at the others. They all seem afraid of him."

"So, there should be no one upstairs," said Willie reflectively. "Can you get to the roof, Duncan?"

Before he could answer, the front door opened and the men started to file out. "One, two," Willie counted quietly, "three, and Sinn." The door closed, then opened again. "Five, six," Willie continued. "That leaves Sleat alone. Very strange. Sleat must be desperate and wants everyone hunting for you."

The six men disappeared into the darkness.

"I'll try the roof," said Duncan. "Jeanne can watch from over there, and if I get inside she will tell you. Then I want you to try to break in the front door. Be careful. Sleat may fire through the door. I just want him to be sufficiently alarmed to retreat upstairs. I don't want him escaping from anywhere on the ground floor. It's time for our final meeting. Sleat and I must settle things one way or the other."

Jeanne shivered, for there was an edge to the quiet voice that was more frightening than any of Heli's ghost stories.

He picked up the rope, and Angus handed him a bundle tied with a leather sling. "A rapier, a claymore, and a pistol with powder and shot, with the captain's compliments."

"You are a credit to your clan, Angus. When I get inside, count a slow hundred before you start." He put the bundle over his shoulder and moved quickly to the far side of the house. Jeanne slipped across to the edge of the cliff to wait for him to appear on the roof.

A drift of clouds blew across the face of the new moon, and Jeanne watched the black outline of the roof come and go against the changing sky. Then she saw Duncan's figure etched on the roofline. He swung over the edge and lowered himself, clearly visible now against the pale wall. When he reached the door there was a rasping noise from high on the roof, and some stones in the chimney around which he had tied the rope began to break off. A shower of stones bounced off Duncan, making short sharp cracks as they hit the rocks far below. She saw him wipe his brow and tug again at the door. It opened suddenly and swung him out away from the house. As he swung back he jumped inside. She saw his hand wave, and he pulled the door closed.

She ran back to the waiting shadows. "He's inside."

Willie began counting slowly to one hundred.

"... ninety-nine, one hundred. Right, Angus, we go to work now. Jeanne, you watch the side and the back of the house. We don't want Sleat getting away. If you see any sign of him, make enough noise to make him think we have the house surrounded and scare him back inside."

Angus picked up a broken beam from the ruins and followed Willie across the street to Sleat's front door. "Just a little battering ram," he explained.

Willie tested the door and found it locked. "It's probably bolted. Give it a tap with your battering ram, Angus. But keep it gentle. We don't want the door down yet, or Sleat may blow our heads off."

Angus gave a tap that almost shook the house. The door splintered but didn't break, and they heard Sleat rush into the hallway.

"Whoever you are, if you make another move to enter this house, I'll put a bullet through you," he shouted.

"You have misspent your last bullet. The boy's friends have come to see to that. The house is surrounded."

Willie motioned to Angus to stand out of the line of fire.

"Damn your eyes, Willie. I'd recognize that voice anywhere." A shot ripped through the door.

"There are too many ways for us to get in," Willie called. "Don't waste your powder."

The candlelight that had filtered through the cracks in the splintered panel disappeared.

"He's backing up the stairs. He thinks he can hold us off from the top. Knock that panel out and I'll fire through." Willie brandished his musket. "Even if I don't hit him, I should at least drive him toward Duncan."

Angus drove the beam at the door and Willie fired.

Sleat fell up the stairs in his rush to escape. He reached the second floor, looking for a secure place to hold out until help arrived. The candle had blown out when he tripped on the stairs and he felt his way along the hall in the darkness. He came to the edge of a doorway and remembered the room where his men slept. With a choked cry of relief, he opened the door, slammed it shut and slid the bolt. He turned, leaned back against the door—and found himself staring at Duncan Macpherson.

Duncan sat at a table, holding a pistol. The candles glinted off a rapier and a claymore set out before him.

"Well Sleat, after all these years of searching, you have finally found me. Not quite right though, is it? Not exactly as you planned. Throw your pistols across the floor under the table, or I'll shoot you where you stand."

Sleat was silent. His face was expressionless. Only his eyes were wild and staring, like those of a cornered animal. Then, almost casually, he pulled a second pistol from his coat and threw both weapons across the floor. Duncan laid his pistol on the table.

"What is your pleasure, rapier or claymore?"

"I'd be a fool to choose the claymore against a man who has survived by it, and you would be a fool to challenge me with the rapier. But you always were a fool, Macpherson, so you should die one." Sleat unsheathed his rapier and Duncan picked up the rapier that lay on the table.

Slowly, the two men began to circle each other in the middle of the room, flexing the swords, waiting for the first thrust.

Then Sleat attacked. He drove his enemy back across the room until Duncan, with a skill and venom that matched his own, counterattacked. Sleat was forced back and the fight became attack and counterattack between equals in skill and determination.

They heard a crash from downstairs—Willie and Angus had decided the time had come to smash the door down. This made Sleat redouble his efforts, but gradually Duncan began to gain the upper hand. Sleat's thrusts became more desperate, less accurate. Duncan drew first blood with a thrust that pierced Sleat's left shoulder. With a snarl of pain, Sleat spun around and snatched up Duncan's pistol from the table.

He cocked it and fired. Nothing.

"I didn't bother to load it," said Duncan.

Sleat threw the pistol in his face and looked frantically around for a way to escape. Relentlessly, Duncan moved toward him. Sleat slashed with his rapier in rage as he backed away. He could retreat no further. His back was against a door. He reached behind him, found the handle and turned it. The door opened. With a cry of fury and relief he hurled his rapier at Duncan. "This time you win, but I'll hunt you down again." He stepped backwards. Duncan shouted a warning but ducked to avoid Sleat's rapier, and his words were lost. He heard a scream falling into the night and rushed to the open doorway. Sleat's body lay spread-eagled on the rocks below.

The pounding on the inner door grew louder. With a last look below, Duncan unbolted it to find Angus, Willie, and behind them, Jeanne, waiting anxiously. He pointed to the door swinging out to the void.

"Be careful."

As they looked down, they saw a figure moving across the rocks. It bent over the sprawled body. Then it looked up.

"Is it you, Macpherson?"

Duncan stood, silhouetted in the doorway. "Aye, Sinn. Is it over, then?"

"It is over," called the singsong voice.

As he carried Sleat's body away, Sinn called up to them again. "Look to your son now Duncan Macpherson. A dark fate may still be following you. He will be tried tomorrow."

The Trial

September 1759

Early next morning a small anxious group collected in Heli's cellar. Willie had leave by the admiral's permission, Angus and Duncan had obtained passes from their captains. "It would be a sorry end to the day to have Jamie free and his father under arrest for being absent without leave," said Duncan. "Still, it is a new experience for me to do things by the rules."

Madame Carrière wanted to be a witness, but Heli pointed out that "it would not do the boy a service to praise him for helping Canadians."

"Only Angus and me have any hope of being at the court martial," said Willie. "We can claim to be witnesses. It's to be held on the admiral's ship this morning. Jamie has already been taken aboard. We'll get word to you as soon as we can."

Duncan walked down to the river with them. "It will be torture to wait here, but needs must." He pushed them off in the rowboat that Madame Carrière had found for them.

"Witnesses for the court martial," Willie called to the watch on deck when they reached the *Princess Amelia*. "Permission to come aboard."

Once on deck, they went to the Great Cabin but were stopped by the guard at the door. "No one allowed in without the admiral's permission as an official witness."

Just then Surgeon Wackley came along. He brightened at the sight of them. "These men are needed to support my testimony." He waved his summons as a witness in front of the guard. "Follow me," he ordered, and all three men marched past the surprised guard.

A long table had been placed at one end of the Great Cabin with chairs for the judges. Parchment, pens, and a silver inkstand were set out in front of the high-backed chair at the centre of the table. Candles burning in silver candlesticks were placed at intervals along the table. The chair for the accused sat alone in the middle of the floor, facing the judges. Seats for the witnesses were lined up at the back near the door. The room began to fill up with officers of the fleet.

"What happens now, Willie?" The surgeon settled himself down. "You have always struck me as a man who would be experienced in courts martial."

"It isn't my first," Willie agreed. "Whatever happens, don't go antagonizing the judges. Remember that this court wants to hang Jamie. They'll consider any other verdict to be a wasted opportunity to send a warning to the navy."

"I hope it isn't as cut and dried as that." Wackley shifted uneasily in his chair.

"They'll be fair," Willie muttered, half to himself. "The admiral will demand that, but they go by the book—so don't hope for too much."

The door at the far end of the Great Cabin opened and a guard came in followed by a very nervous Jamie, who was led to the prisoner's chair. He looked around and they could see his spirits rise when he noticed his small band of friends. He straightened up and stood with more confidence.

The judges entered and everyone stood while they filed in to take their places at the long table. After all were seated, the ranking officer spoke.

"This court is now in session. Read the charges against the prisoner."

A ruddy-faced officer stood up and bowed to the bench. "My Lords."

The judge interrupted him. "This isn't the Old Bailey, sir. Get on with it."

The officer's face grew even redder. "The charges against the prisoner, Jamie Macpherson, are that he is a French spy and that he did desert from the King's service in time of war. Both crimes being punishable by death." He sat down.

"How does the prisoner plead?" asked the judge.

"Not guilty, sir. On both counts," said Jamie. He spoke

in a low voice, but Willie was glad to hear the firm tone. He nodded encouragement.

"I don't see how anyone could be guilty on both counts," said the judge. "Can you explain this?"

"The charges were laid in a letter by two midshipmen of the *Princess Amelia* who were captured on Île aux Coudres," said the prosecutor. "The accused went ashore with the midshipmen, but when they were captured by a group of Canadians, the accused was not taken prisoner. He was accepted by the Canadians as one of them. He spoke French, sir, and conversed with them."

"Good God, man," interrupted the judge. "I speak French. Am I to be regarded as a spy? What do you say to this charge of spying?" He glowered at Jamie.

"I was press-ganged into the navy in Glasgow, and the men who were press-ganged with me are here as witnesses," said Jamie. He pointed to Willie and Angus. "We tried to explain that we shouldn't be in the navy, and we asked to be discharged, but the navy refused. I was a loblolly boy for Surgeon Wackley. I never had anything to spy about. I don't know a single secret of the British navy."

"Does this sound like a spy?" The judge glowered in turn at the embarrassed prosecutor.

"Sir, I would like to drop the charge of spying and, with your leave, I will prove that the prisoner is a deserter in time of war," said the prosecutor, scrabbling through his papers.

"This case had better be more convincing," said the judge coldly.

The prosecutor nodded and continued. "The accused left the *Princess Amelia* in the company of the midshipmen to spend a few hours on Île aux Coudres. A few hours at most, sir, but he did not wear his naval clothes. Instead he made up a cock-and-bull story about having just washed them and having to wear his own clothes which would permit him to blend in with the local population. He also took all his belongings wrapped in a blanket. Are these the actions of a boy who intends to return to the ship in a few hours?"

He paused to let this sink into the minds of the judges, and Surgeon Wackley jumped to his feet.

"Sir, I am a surgeon on this ship and I gave the boy permission to go ashore. I told him to take the blanket. I..."

The judge interrupted. "Sit down, Surgeon. We may hear from you later. Continue."

The prosecutor had regained his confidence. He knew that he was on firm ground with the charge of desertion, and that he had the judges' attention. "When the midshipmen were captured, the accused described himself to them as a French boy from Bic, captured by the British when they took on the Canadian pilots at Bic. He disowned his comrades. When he arrived in Quebec, he went to live with a Canadian family and worked for a fishwife. In other words he deserted."

"What do you say in your defence, boy?"

"I did tell the militia captain that I was from Bic, but only because I thought I could escape later and go back to the ship for help."

"Is it true that you did not try once to escape from your captors?" the prosecutor asked with a look of triumph.

"That's true, but…"

"And is it also true that you did not once try to escape from Quebec?"

"Yes, but…" Jamie was becoming flustered.

"The court should know that not only did the accused never attempt to return to his ship while the war continued, but that even after our forces were victorious he continued to remain with the French. Are these the actions of a poor victim of circumstances who wishes to escape at the first opportunity and rejoin his ship to fight for his King and Country? Or are these the actions of a deserter who fears to return to his just punishment?"

The prosecutor paused to give emphasis to his conclusion. "I respectfully submit that the accused is guilty of desertion in time of war."

The Great Cabin was silent. The judge then spoke directly to Jamie. "You have heard the evidence, and it is convincing. Do you have anything to say in your defence before we pass judgment?"

Jamie looked hunted. "I…"

There was a scuffle at the door, angry words from the guard and then, "May I have the permission of the court to speak?" A voice came from the back of the room.

"Come forward and state your business," said the judge.

Sinn strode forward and stood before him.

Jamie had never seen Sinn like this. He looked every inch the respectable merchant. His slouching manner had been replaced by an upright, confident attitude. Only his eyes remained as before. Their pale gaze swept over the officers and settled on the judge.

"My name is Sinn," he said. "I am a merchant in the service of the King. I have been engaged in shipping supplies to the army, and I have also been looking for this boy. I would not presume to interfere in the affairs of the court, but the honourable judges would wish to be informed that the accused is not a sailor in the King's service. These letters show that he was discharged months ago. I have been looking for him to deliver these letters as a small service to his uncle, Archibald Gilchrist, an old friend of mine."

Willie didn't know whether he wanted to shake Sinn's hand or wring his neck. "The old devil," he whispered to Wackley. "But he might just save Jamie's life."

Sinn continued as the judge inspected the letters of discharge. "It would be a strange denial of the King's wishes to hang the boy as a deserter."

The judge looked up from the papers. "Case dismissed. The papers are in order." He walked over to Jamie, "I hope you never come as close to being hanged again. I can tell you one thing now, the admiral will be better pleased with this outcome than the one I had in mind a moment ago."

Jamie's row of supporters gave a suppressed cheer. Angus and the surgeon went quickly to him, and Willie went over to thank Sinn.

"I don't know how or why you did it, but I'm grateful."

"I've come into a little good fortune," said Sinn. "Let

me buy you a drink and tell you about it. Where can we go?"

"We'll take Jamie to his father and go to the old fortune-teller's house in what's left of Lower Town. Come with us. Duncan will be as surprised as I am."

"I'll join you there later. I think it would be safer if Duncan knows I mean him no harm before we meet again."

"Do you know where Heli's house is?"

Sinn smiled. "The one with the little red cat and the black-haired girl. I know it well. Now I have some business with the admiral."

Willie went over to Jamie who was describing his ordeal to the others. "Well lad, not to interrupt, but we have one more surprise for you, and we must go ashore to find it."

As Angus rowed, Surgeon Wackley sat rigidly in the centre of the boat proclaiming that if God had meant man to travel on water he would have given him webbed feet. Jamie leaned back in the bow, looking at the clouds scudding across the sky.

"If you can stop gazing at the sky," Willie said, "there is someone waiting for you." He pointed to the tall, anxious figure that waited on the dock.

"Father!"

A stream of Gaelic echoed across the water, and Angus almost lifted the boat out of the water as he bent the oars to cover the last few yards to the shore.

Duncan reached out and gave a hand to Jamie who leapt ashore. They hugged each other.

"It has been a longer road than I expected, but it is well ended," Duncan said, and still holding Jamie, he shook hands all around as they climbed ashore. "Thank you all. I am in your debt forever."

"The strange thing is, that the one who saved the lad was Sinn," said Willie. "Trouble brings you odd allies, but none could be odder than Sinn."

While they walked back toward Heli's he described the court martial to Duncan.

Jamie ran ahead, but the word of his release raced even faster along Champlain Street, and everyone who had come back cheered and waved as he sped to Heli and Jeanne who were coming to meet him.

"Not a spy. Not a thief. Not even a sailor," he gasped when he reached them. Jamie was so pleased to be back among friends in Heli's house that he couldn't stop grinning and looking from one to another. He and Jeanne sat on the floor beside Heli's rocking chair. Madame Carrière and Heli were talking to Surgeon Wackley. Angus was pouring Duncan a dram of his precious water of life and talking about Skye with a blissful faraway look on his face.

Willie lounged by the door, stroking Fergie and watching the street. Soon a bent figure in a floppy black hat slouched along and sat on a bench in front of Madame Carrière's house. Willie went over to him. "I recognize you better in these clothes. Now tell me how you came by Jamie's discharge papers."

Sinn tilted back his hat and enjoyed the sun on his face. "I gave the papers to Sleat months ago and forgot all about them until last night. When I took his body for burial I went through his pockets and found them. We had a strange relationship because of the years we had known each other, but that's a long story, so let me get back to last night. I went through his pockets because I needed papers myself to get back to Scotland. I didn't want to end up like Jamie, accused of desertion in a war I'd never agreed to fight. We were here on a mercantile arrangement which suited his Majesty and profited Sleat, and I needed documents that would let me bluff my way back onto one of Sleat's ships. That's when I found the boy's discharge papers. I also found a letter from Sleat—to me. In it he spends three pages telling me what a rogue and a thief I am, and then he makes me the sole heir to his estate. It's duly witnessed and a copy has been deposited with a lawyer in Glasgow."

As Willie shook his head in disbelief, Sinn continued. "I told you he was a strange one. Now he has turned me into a rich man. What do you think of that, Willie? Doesn't that destroy your faith in justice."

Willie sighed. "You get changed from a common rogue to a gentleman rogue, and I'm stuck in the King's navy, three thousand miles from the nearest Glasgow tavern. There's no justice."

"Such self-pity," said Sinn, "and on such a happy occasion too. Oh well, I had to give it to you sometime and it might as well be now."

He threw a package in Willie's lap. "I found discharge papers for you too, and I've persuaded the admiral to sign your release. I have a ship sailing tomorrow, and I'll even guarantee you safe passage."

Willie stared at the letter of discharge. "Safe passage. Straight to Glasgow?"

Sinn nodded. "You have my word as a rogue and a gentleman."

Willie beamed and they shook hands on it.

"Take this with you," said Sinn as Willie got up to go and tell the others. "It's a poor celebration without provisions." He pointed to the sack he had been carrying.

Willie swung it over his shoulder. "Come with me," he said. "Duncan wants to thank you for saving Jamie." But Sinn was already halfway down the street.

Willie returned to the house and deposited the sack at Heli's feet. "A present from the Devil so be careful how you sup." He turned to Jamie with a wide, broken-toothed smile, "I'm discharged, and with a fair wind, Fergie and me will be drinking in The Black Bull in the month. Are you coming with me or signing on with the King's navy?"

Jamie looked around the cellar at his friends, half of whom were supposed to be his enemies. "I only had one real enemy," he thought, "and he is dead. I am free to go to Virginia, or Scotland, or Normandy, or anywhere in the world." He looked over to his father. "Where do we go now?"

"Where do you want to go?" asked Duncan.

"Nowhere," said Jamie.

"Then you have arrived," said Heli. "You have made a brave choice. I foresee a long hard winter, but a beautiful spring."

Afterword

Many journals and letters from both sides in the battle for Quebec have survived: from the two generals themselves, Montcalm and Wolfe, from a nun at the General Hospital and another at the Ursulines, from a pilot and from a priest. You can even find out what the weather was like on Thursday, September 13, the date of the battle of the Plains of Abraham: "fresh breezes and cloudy" with "calms and showers" in the middle of the day. If you want to read more about the campaign, Captain John Knox's *Journal* gives a vivid description from a British officer's point of view.

There are many paintings and engravings of the city too, done by soldier-artists with Wolfe's army and later on by members of the garrison.

There really was an Admiral Durell and three (or perhaps two) midshipmen were captured in June on Île aux Coudres. The early accounts say that one of them was either a nephew, son or grandson of the admiral. Their names are given in the ship's log of the *Princess Amelia*— George Douglas, La Maite and Viat. St. Barbe. And in 1716 on Champlain Street, there was a fortune teller called Heli. We like to think that it was Jeanne's grandfather, just beginning his career.

We first learned of the capture of the midshipmen in a forgotten book called *The Little Admiral* by Jean McIlwraith, a Canadian writer. She also wrote a book for adults called *The Span o'life* (with W. MacLennan), set in the same period.

Some of the street names are different nowadays, but Quebec remains much as Jamie and Jeanne knew it. The Chateau Frontenac Hotel now stands on the site of the Chateau St. Louis which burnt down in 1834. The Récollets' monastery was replaced by Trinity Cathedral in 1818. But there are still artisan's shops on rue Petit-Champlain, and l'Hôpital général where the refugees found shelter still cares for the sick. If you visit the Ursuline Convent you can see Montcalm's skull.

It's not hard to dream yourself into the past as you walk around the old walled city or stand on the ramparts looking at the river and the mountains beyond.

bannock: a round, flat, unsweetened cake, usually made from oats or barley and baked on a griddle (a heavy flat pan)

bulkhead: walls dividing any area between two decks into separate rooms

Canadian pilots: the river pilots from Bic were Canadian. At this time, the inhabitants of New France were known as the Canadians.

claymore: a large two-edged broadsword used by Scottish Highlanders. The single-edged basket-hilted sword used later is also often called a claymore.

collicks: colic (severe pains in the stomach)

cross-trees: timbers at the upper end of the lower masts which support the frame of the upper mast

dirk: a dagger used by the Highlanders

dragoon: a mounted infantryman armed with a carbine

garret: attic

gauntlet: to "run the gauntlet" was an army, navy or school punishment where the victim had to pass between two rows of men who would strike him with sticks. As used in the story it means to go through a situation of great danger.

gibbet: gallows

Glaswegian: a person who comes from Glasgow; the dialect of someone from Glasgow

grenadier: originally a foot soldier who threw grenades. Later a company of elite soldiers in an infantry regiment.

grogseller: someone who sells grog (watered rum, known as "the sailor's best friend")

habitant: a Canadian farmer of New France

High Kirk: the main Church of Scotland church in a town or area

Highland: the mountainous region in the north of Scotland; something typical of the area

Iroquois: an important group of North American Indian tribes

Jacobite: a supporter of the Stuart claimants to the British throne after 1688

loblolly: assistant to a surgeon on board a ship

midshipman: a young man in training aboard ship for a commission in the Royal Navy

nobs: slang for people of wealth and high rank

orlop deck: lowest deck of ship

plaid: a long piece of tartan cloth worn over one shoulder as part of Highland costume

press'd: to be seized and forced to serve in the navy

press-ganged: to be taken by the press gang, a group of sailors from a ship led by an officer

pressing tender: the vessel that held the people captured until they were assigned to a commissioned ship

ramparts: walls built around a city to defend it

rapier: a small light sword

rapscallion: a rogue or rascal

Récollets: a branch of the Franciscan order who first came to Quebec in 1615

sally port: an opening in a wall for the besieged to rush out (sally forth) and attack their besiegers

smiddy: a blacksmith's workshop

tansy: a tall bitter herb with yellow buttonlike flowers and feathery leaves

the great cabin: the senior officer's cabin

Traverse: a channel on the St. Lawrence River east of Île d'Orléans

Ursulines: nuns of an order founded in 1535 to nurse the sick and educate girls. They came to Quebec in 1639, and are there still.

The verse Jamie recites is taken from *Carmina Gadelica*, a collection of songs, chants and hymns Alexander Carmichael translated from the Gaelic. (p. 119)

Further references:
  Collins Gem Scots Dictionary
  Falconer's Marine Dictionary (1780 ed.)

Together John and Mary Alice Downie have visited many of the places Jamie travelled to in the novel.

They have journeyed to Normandy to see the village where the story begins, camped in Bic, visited Île aux Coudres, and wandered through Quebec City—Lower and Upper Town, the Ursuline Convent, the General Hospital.

On their sojourns, Mary Alice writes travel articles and John takes the photographs.

Much of *Danger in Disguise* was written during a sabbatical year in Cambridge, England, where the couple were surrounded by eighteenth century buildings and once dined at a Georgian feast at King's College.

John was born and raised in Glasgow. He wasn't press-ganged but came to Canada of his own free will after graduating from university. He is an engineer by profession and frequently edits Mary Alice's projects.

Mary Alice was born in Illinois, of Canadian parents, and grew up in Toronto. Her extensive credits include anthologies for children and adults, picture books, and fantasies and historical novels for both older and younger children. She is also well established in the publishing community as a critic, editor and re-teller of folktales.

CANADIAN HISTORICAL FICTION FROM ROUSSAN

CANDLES, Lynne Kositsky
DARK OF THE MOON, Barbara Haworth-Attard
HOME CHILD, Barbara Haworth-Attard
LIVING FREIGHT, Dayle Campbell Gaetz
RUN FOR YOUR LIFE, Wilma E. Alexander
SUNFLOWER DIARY, Lillian Boraks-Nemetz
THE VIRTUAL ZONE, Lynda Wilson:
 IN SEARCH OF KLONDIKE GOLD
 TITANIC'S RACE TO DISASTER